Dead in the Creek

A Henry Walsh Mystery

Gregory Payette

8 Flags Publishing, Inc.

DEAD IN THE CREEK

Sign up for the newsletter on my website:

GregoryPayette.com

Once or twice a month I'll send you updates and news. Plus, you'll be the first to hear about new releases with special prices. If you'd like to receive the Henry Walsh prequel (for free) use the sign-up form here:

GregoryPayette.com/crossroad

Chapter 1

I LEANED WITH MY arms crossed on the rail around the edge of Friendship Fountain. The jets blasted water at least a hundred feet into the air and a cool mist dropped down onto my face. My mind went somewhere else for a couple of moments, although it didn't help I hadn't even had a sip of coffee.

I straightened up off the rail and turned, looking around. Nothing.

It looked like my prospective client was a no-show.

The details Sarah Jenner had shared with me on the phone the night before were lacking. The truth was, there *were* no details. She didn't say why she wanted to hire us, and only briefly mentioned her husband. The call was short. And she promised to share the details when we met.

I turned back to the fountain and gazed up at the water sprayed into the air, then shifted my eyes to the St. Johns behind it. There was something about the spraying, splashing sounds of a fountain.

There was something about water.

I wondered if Sarah Jenner had something to do with an affair. But my partner Alex and I had sworn off cases that involved cheating spouses. The money was decent, but they weren't worth the headaches. For whatever reason, clients with cheating spouses tended to have more money than they knew what to do with. And with that came demands we often had to refuse. I'd only recently dodged a lawsuit for invasion of privacy, and it would've cost me my business if my friend Billy hadn't had a lawyer friend help make it go away.

But business had been slow. And Sarah Jenner sounded nice enough on the phone. I was also somewhat intrigued not by what she said, but by what she *didn't* say.

My phone rang on my walk back to the parking lot.

It was Alex. "Where are you?"

I stepped inside my Jeep and slid the key in the ignition. "Leaving Friendship Fountain. Sarah Jenner didn't show up."

Alex was quiet for a moment. "Henry, I just got a call. Sarah Jenner is dead."

I paused, unsure I heard correctly, then asked a useless question. "What do you mean, she's dead?"

"Her car went off the road early this morning."

"On her way here?"

"No. They believe it happened around dawn. A jogger found her car just south of San Marco, at the bottom of an embankment...partly submerged in a creek."

My phone conversation the night before with Sarah was two minutes long. If that. No, I didn't know her or anything about her. But for some reason, I felt it. At least at that moment when Alex said she'd been killed. Maybe it was a sense of guilt. But I wasn't sure why."

"Who told you?" I said.

"Her sister called the office, said she knew her sister had talked about hiring us. But she didn't know why."

"That makes two of us."

I slid the key into the ignition and backed out of the parking space, hit the gas hard and turned onto San Marco Boulevard. I still had the phone up to my ear. "Strange the sister called us, don't you think?"

"Strange? In what way?"

I thought for a moment. "Her sister was just killed, and she's worried about letting a stranger know why she missed her appointment?"

. . . • • . • • . . .

Our office was just above Billy's Place, my good friend Billy Wu's restaurant. It's where I spent a good part of my days and many nights. It was convenient, since I could work and eat and drink and walk home to my boat in the marina not even a mile away.

Alex looked up at me from her desk when I walked through the door. "Sarah Jenner's sister called again. She wants to meet."

I stared back at Alex. "What that's supposed to mean?" I stepped toward the coffee machine and picked up the pot, gave it a sniff. "Is this from today?"

"I just made it. Figured you'd need some."

I poured myself a coffee and sat down at my desk, reaching for the wooden bin with a stack of mail. It was all bills. A lot of them. Unpaid, of course.

Alex got up and walked toward my desk. She stood over me with her arms crossed. "She said she wants to talk to us. About the accident."

I tossed the bills back in the bin. "I hate to sound insensitive, but if we don't land a new client..." I sipped my coffee and leaned back in my chair.

"That's a little cold, isn't it?"

"The coffee?" I shook my head, but knew what she meant.

Alex gave me a look. "A woman's dead, Henry. And all you can think about is that we need a new client?"

I rolled my eyes. "You know me better than that." I looked down at the pile of bills. "I'm sorry about what happened to

Mrs. Jenner. *Of course* I am. But..." I shrugged. "You're right. It's all just—"

My cell phone rang, which at that point in my conversation with Alex seemed to be good timing. "This is Henry."

A woman's voice spoke on the other end, "Is this Henry Walsh?"

"It is." There was silence on the other end. I looked at my screen to check the number then put the phone back to my ear. "Can I help you?"

"My name is Melinda Hill. I understand you were supposed to meet my sister Sarah this morning? I spoke to a woman at your office earlier and she gave me this number and..."

"Yes, Alex told me you called. I'm very sorry about your sister. I'm still in disbelief. Although I only spoke to her briefly last night, I...I can't imagine how you must feel right now."

"No, you can't." She paused. "Did she tell you why she wanted to hire you?"

"To be honest, no. She didn't. I suppose I thought it had something to do with her husband. But she wasn't clear about it. She didn't give me any details."

"It's a little suspicious, don't you think?"

I hesitated a moment. "I'm sorry?"

"I just...I can't help but believe he had something to do with what happened to her."

"*Who* had something to do with *what*?"

"Sarah's husband, Jeffrey. I'm afraid he might've had something to do with the accident."

"Hold on a moment," I said. "Are you saying her husband is responsible for her death? Have you mentioned this to anyone at the sheriff's office?"

"They already bounced me around from one officer to another when I called. Said they'd take a statement but nobody's called me back."

"Did you go by the station?"

Melinda was quiet on the other end for a moment. "Please, Mr. Walsh. I'd like to meet with you. I don't have a lot of money, but I'd like to hire you to investigate what happened. If I have to sell everything I own to pay you, I will. I just want the truth."

I was quiet for a moment. "We can meet first, before we get into any of the financial details. In the meantime, we'll make some calls. My partner has connections at the Sheriff's Office...we'll try to get some answers before you commit to anything."

"I can meet tomorrow at noon. If it's all right, my office isn't far from Friendship Fountain. I can meet you there, on my lunch break."

I don't know if she knew that's where I was supposed to meet Sarah, or if it was just a coincidence. But the whole thing felt a little odd. In fact the whole day felt strange. I sipped my coffee and wiggled the mouse on my computer. I looked at my calendar and, other than my planned meeting with Sarah a few hours earlier, it was completely empty.

Chapter 2

Alex looked up from her phone and turned to me from the passenger seat of my Jeep. "Sarah was on her way to the gym to meet a friend. Her husband, Jeffrey Jenner, had already gone to work. He didn't know what time she'd left."

"Did he go into work the same time he always did?" I glanced over at Alex.

She shrugged. "How would I know that?"

I turned my eyes back to the road and drove across the Main Street Bridge and over the St. Johns. We turned onto Museum Circle and parked.

We walked toward the fountain and I said, "Strange Melinda's at work today. The day after her sister's killed."

Alex glanced at me, but didn't respond.

I spotted a woman with her back to us, facing the fountain. The way she dressed made her stand out from the runners and mothers chasing their children around in circles.

We walked up behind her. "Melinda?"

The woman turned, wearing sunglasses, and reached out to shake my hand. "Melinda Hill," she said.

"I'm Henry. And this is Alex."

Alex said, "Henry said your office is nearby?"

She nodded. "Not too far. I work for P.A.S."

"What's that?" I said.

"One of the largest pharmaceutical companies in the world. I've been there six years," She smiled, tight-lipped. "Still trying to crash through the glass ceiling, but it hasn't gone exactly as planned. Not when the men who run the company are intimidated by strong-minded women."

Alex and I exchanged a look. It sounded to me like she had some hostility toward her job. Or maybe toward the men. Which I guess I understood.

The three of us walked along the fountain and sat at one of the free tables.

I sat next to Alex, across from Melinda. "Would you like to start by telling us why you believe Jeffrey Jenner had something to do with your sister's accident?"

"For starters," she said, "I told you I'm not convinced it was an accident. But there's also the fact Jeffrey was cheating on her. It was brutally obvious. I'm not even sure why she thought she needed a private investigator to prove it."

"But I thought you weren't sure why she wanted to hire us?" I said.

Melinda shook her head. "She told me she'd tell me the details after she met with you." She looked down toward the table. "Jeffrey was sleeping with a young woman from his firm. I'm almost certain of it."

"*Almost* certain?" I said.

"Jeffrey's an architect. Sarah said he'd work late into the night. Or some days he'd be out of the house before the sun was up." She rolled her eyes. "I told her it was a clear sign..."

Alex said, "She never witnessed anything?"

"I thought that's why she called you?" She looked down at her phone. "I'm sorry, but I only have a few minutes before I have to get back. I should've brought my lunch..."

I said, "We don't know if that's why Sarah called us."

Melinda shifted in her seat. "She didn't tell you?"

I shook my head. "Our call was brief."

Melinda looked away for a moment, gazing toward the fountain. "Can I hire you to find out what happened to Sarah? If my suspicions are correct, the trail will lead you right to Jeffrey. And I'll be sure he pays for what he did to my sister."

Alex glanced at me and said to Melinda, "But, of course, there's a cost involved. And if you don't have a lot of money... What if the sheriff's office concludes it was nothing more than a tragic accident? If we just give them a little more time, it may not be necessary to hire us before they—"

"I'm not going to wait for their investigation to finish." Melinda stared back at Alex then shifted her gaze to mine. "You know how it is with things like this, don't you? A car goes off the road in the early morning, looks pretty cut-and-dry that it's an accident, right? Of course, if the police investigation leans in that direction, that it was an accident, nobody'll do the extra wor to prove otherwise. Am I right?"

I wasn't about to turn away a paying client. But I didn't have a good feeling about this one. A man may be a cheater, but it doesn't make him a killer.

"There are no guarantees," I said. "As long as you understand that. And, of course, we get paid for our time. But you won't be tied to a contract or anything like that. If our investigation gets to a point where you don't feel it's in your best interest to continue, you'll only have to pay us for our time." I looked past Melinda, toward the fountain. "If either Alex or I feel the case doesn't have legs, we'll let you know." I looked her in the eye. "You won't have to spend money you don't have to."

She folded her hands on the table. "I can afford to pay you for a little more than a week. Maybe two weeks, if you feel it'll take that long."

Alex and I both stared straight ahead at Melinda.

"Well, that's not a lot of time," I said. "Of course, we always work as fast as we can. But, the truth is, there's a lot involved in a case like this." I gave Alex a look and she nodded before I turned back to Melinda. "We'll take the case. And we'll do everything in our power to find the truth about what happened to your sister."

· · · · ● · ● · ● · · ·

Billy put a beer down on the bar in front of me and wiped his hands on the towel draped over his shoulder. He leaned down with both hands on the bar. "I saw the accident on the news...the back-end of the car was stuck straight up in the air." He turned and looked at the other patrons along the bar "They found her outside the car...in the water?"

I nodded. "Investigators think she might've been hurt, maybe climbed out the open window before the car sank in the creek."

Billy turned to walk away but stopped and looked back at me. "I know you told her you'd take the case. But if she puts a time limit on it because she can't afford more than a week or two? You're the last person who'll put on the brakes on something without an answer." He shook his head. "You wouldn't sleep a minute knowing you didn't have a resolution."

Alex looked up from her laptop.

I shrugged. "We have bills to pay. We'll do what we can do. But it's not like we can afford to work for free once we're no longer being paid."

Billy huffed out a laugh. "You say that now. But how many people have you helped without asking for a dime?" He sipped his coffee and looked at me over the rim of his cup then walked away, poured two draft beers from the tap and carried them down the bar. He was back a moment later, stopped in front of me and again leaned with his hands down on the bar. "Is a young girlfriend on the side enough to murder your wife?" He turned over his shoulder and looked toward the kitchen. His head cook Jake walked out with a plate in each hand. Billy said, "Did I tell you Jake went to school with the Jenner's son?"

I shook my head and looked at Jake, coming up behind Billy.

He stepped toward us and put two plates down on the bar in front of me and Alex. Jake smiled. "Enjoy it." He started back toward the kitchen, but I called for him and he turned.

I waved him over. Jake, Billy said you know Sarah Jenner's son?"

He nodded. "Yeah, I know Wyatt. We went to school together." He walked back toward us then glanced at Billy. "Actually, Chloe and I are going to the service tomorrow, so I'll be gone for a few hours. I hope that's okay." He pointed over his shoulder with his thumb. "Roy's going to come in early...he should be able to handle the lunch rush while I'm gone."

Chloe was Jake's fiancé and also Billy's only other bartender. She'd recently graduated from JU and Billy was afraid she'd be leaving soon for what some might call a 'real job.'

"So you know Wyatt pretty well?" I said.

Jake shrugged. "I guess. Not like I used to, but Chloe said we should go. I'm not big on going to things like that; funerals or wakes or..."

"Who *is*?" I said. "So you must know his family?"

Jake shrugged. "A little." He grabbed a glass and filled it with soda from the gun. "His mom used to go to all his games. But his dad wasn't around much." Jake smiled. "We all used to joke about how hot Mrs. Jenner was."

Alex rolled her eyes and the smile left Jake's face. "Oh, I'm sorry. I shouldn't joke about it like that now. But she was really nice. We all liked her."

I sipped my beer. "How's he doing?"

"He's been away at school, so I haven't really talked to him. I guess I'll find out tomorrow. I'll let you know."

I thought for a moment. "Actually, I might be there." I took a bite of my sandwich.

Jake had a puzzled look on his face. "I didn't know you knew her."

I wiped my mouth with the napkin and took a drink. "She was almost a client. Although we never actually met face-to-face." As soon as the words left my mouth I knew I shouldn't have said a word. I said to Jake, "Do me a favor, pretend I didn't just say that. Or, at least keep it to yourself."

He said, "You mean that you knew Wyatt's mom?"

I nodded. "Yeah, that would be good."

Jake nodded and wiped his hands on his apron. He looked nervous. "You don't have to worry about me saying a thing." He turned and looked back toward the kitchen. "I'd better get back in there."

Billy looked up at the clock on the wall at the back of the bar. The place started to get busy, without a single empty stool. "I wonder if Jake knows where Chloe is? I'm getting too old to handle a bar rush by myself."

Chapter 3

Melinda showed up at our office at seven-thirty sharp and stepped through the door. "I didn't know your office was above a restaurant."

"At least we have our own entrance now. You used to have to cut through the kitchen to get up here." I didn't tell her about the stained carpets and the dirty couch you wouldn't sit on unless you were up to date on your shots. Not to mention the odors from the kitchen that never went away.

But that was before Billy's Place was destroyed by an explosion and he rebuilt the entire place, from the ground up. Our new office space had hardwoods and faux leather furniture (Alex would never allow real leather) and even a bathroom with a small shower.

"We can go downstairs and have a drink while we talk, or we can stay right here." I gestured toward the round table with four chairs we had in the corner of the office. We rarely used it.

She nodded toward the couch. "Do you mind if we sit there?"

Melinda had on jeans and a buttoned-down shirt. Like a business woman trying to relax.

I, on the other hand, had no trouble being casual. Shorts and Sperry Topsiders and whatever shirt was clean enough was my normal attire.

I didn't think it was ever a turnoff to clients. If they wanted someone in a suit they'd have to go somewhere else. I let my work do the talking.

I sat down next to Melinda on the couch.

Alex pulled over the chair from her desk and sat across from me and Melinda.

Melinda looked past me, toward the big window overlooking the St. Johns. "You have a nice view," she said. "I work on the lower floor of my building. Some days I don't even know the weather outside unless I look at my phone."

Melinda was quiet for a couple of moments, like she was trying to think of what to say.

I said, "I know Sarah's funeral's in the morning. I know it's a hard time for you. So, I was thinking, maybe if we waited a few days to get started, so you can—"

"No! I don't want to wait. Jeffrey's doing all the arrange-ments, then hosting brunch after the service." She looked toward the floor. "He didn't even want my help. He knows how I feel about him."

I said, "I just want to make sure you're able to think clear enough. I mean, sometimes your emotions can cloud your thoughts, make it hard to be objective."

Melinda stood from the couch, her hands on her hips. She gave Alex a look then stared down at me. "You think I'm here because of my emotions?" She shook her head. "I had hoped you were going to take this a little more seriously." She grabbed her purse from the couch, threw it over her shoulder and headed toward the door.

I jumped up and followed after her. "Melinda!" I said. "Wait. I'm sorry, I just...I know how difficult it can be. Your loss, I mean. Especially when it's something like this. Something that wasn't supposed to happen."

She had her hand on the door's handle. But she turned, with tears in her eyes, and shook her head. "It's not just that it wasn't supposed to happen. But when you know, in your heart, in your gut, that somebody's responsible and you get the feeling nobody wants to believe you."

Alex got up and walked to Melinda and put her hand on her shoulder. "An investigation like this can take an emotional toll on you. And, of course, we have a small window to work without much evidence other than the belief that Sarah's husband was having an affair."

I stepped toward Melinda and Alex. "Don't take it personally," I said. "We always make sure our clients are prepared. It's just best for all parties involved, our emotions are in check before we move forward."

Alex walked Melinda back to the couch and handed her a box of tissues from the coffee table. She walked into the kitchen area and came out with a glass of water for Melinda. "Here." She sat on the couch.

As tough as Alex could be, she had a way about her where she could make anyone feel comfortable, in almost any situation. And we both knew when it was time for her to step-in and take over. Especially when my tell-it-like-it-is approach didn't work.

I sat in the chair across from them. Alex turned with one leg tucked under the other, facing Melinda. "Tell us about Jeffrey Jenner," she said.

Melinda dabbed the corners of her eyes with the tissue, then balled it up in her hand. "Jeffrey works for an architectural firm called LaSalle and King. And about a year ago they hired a young architect. One of the few females they had in the firm." She turned to me. "I don't know how much Sarah told you..."

"Not much at all," I said. "She didn't want to say much over the phone. As you know, of course, we were supposed to meet that morning."

Melinda nodded. "If I repeat anything, let me know."

Alex put her hand on Melinda's thigh. "It's okay if you do. Just tell us everything."

"Well, Sarah started to suspect something was going on with Jeffrey a couple of months ago." She shrugged. "It's not like their marriage was ever on solid ground. But nobody wants to find out their husband has someone else." She looked down at her hands on her lap. "Although, I don't know for sure if Sarah was always faithful herself."

"You think she had an affair?" Alex said.

Melinda shrugged. "Nothing she ever told me. I just had a feeling."

I glanced at Alex and she looked back at me. I said to Melinda, "You wouldn't have a name?"

She shook her head. "No. Like I said, she never mentioned a word to me. She knew I wouldn't approve."

I leaned forward in the chair with my hands folded out in front of me, my elbows down on my knees. "So what about this young architect from Mr. Jenner's office?"

Melinda took a sip from her glass. "Sarah met her at one of their work events around the holidays." She looked off, as if in deep thought. "I don't know when. It might not have been that long ago. But that's when she first started to wonder if something was going on between this woman and Jeffrey. I remember Sarah telling me every time she looked, the young woman's eyes were on Jeffrey."

"I assume there's more to it?" I said.

Melinda nodded. "Sarah went home that night. But Jeffrey insisted he had to stay, since his clients were there. Which would normally be a legitimate excuse."

Alex and I watched Melinda, patiently waiting for more.

"Sarah's at home on her phone, skimming through Facebook or Instagram—one or the other—and sees a picture someone from Jeffrey's office posted. It was a photo of this young woman with Jeffrey together at the bar. Somewhat of an after party, I guess. And the way Sarah had described it, it was far from a normal photo with two coworkers hanging out. He got home at three in the morning, threw all his clothes in the wash and jumped in the shower."

I sat back in the chair. "Nice of him to do laundry, right?" I looked at Melinda. "Did you see the photo?"

She shook her head. "It was taken down that night, before Jeffrey had even come home."

Alex took Melinda's empty glass from her hand, went to the kitchen area and filled it again. She handed the glass to Melinda. "Sounds to me he certainly had something to hide."

Melinda turned to her and nodded. "And that was just the beginning. Next thing, he's suddenly traveling more for work. Business trips for three or four days a week. Of course, this young woman is on his team. He's her boss."

"Does this young woman have a name?" I said.

"Emma. She's barely twenty-four years old." Melinda sipped from her glass. "Sarah followed her on social media, but she was blocked."

"Did Sarah ever bring it up with Jeffrey?"

Melinda shook her head. "No."

"But you said this started a few months back?" Alex said.

"In the winter. Like I said, sometime around the holidays. Or maybe right after."

"So it'd been going on for at least a few months," I said, then glanced at Alex and stood up from the chair. I walked to the window, and with my back to Melinda and Alex, I stared out toward the St. Johns. The sun had started to set. "So proving he was cheating may be simple. But anything beyond that..." I turned from the window. "But it's a long stretch to prove a husband cheated and also killed his own wife."

Chapter 4

Jeffrey Jenner was a thin man of average height. He had slicked-back, dark hair and wore perfectly round glasses that seemed to be a bit small for his face.

Next to him in the receiving line at Sarah's service was a young man I knew right away was their son Wyatt.

There was no casket, which is always my preference. Not that I've ever minded the sight of a dead body, but it never made a lot of sense to me. There was something strange about pumping someone's body with formaldehyde, glutaraldehyde, methanol, humectants, and whatever other solvents are available just to put the deceased on display. People would stand back and comment, "She looks good."

To me, a dead body rarely looked good.

The line moved along. I'd spent most of the time rehearsing in my head what I'd say to this family I'd never met.

You would think someone in my business would be able to take death lightly. Just part of life. But it always gave me an uneasy feeling, especially when faced with those who'd been left behind.

I stood face-to-face with Jeffrey Jenner and extended my hand. "I'm Henry Walsh." I glanced toward Alex with a nod. "This is Alex. I'm very sorry for your loss."

Jeffrey squeezed my hand, not ready to let go, and pulled me in toward him. He looked me in the eye. "Are you a friend of Sarah's?"

I hesitated a moment, then nodded. "Yes." I pulled my hand away and turned toward Wyatt, shook his hand and put my free hand on his shoulder. "I'm sorry for your loss."

Wyatt gave me a nod. "Thank you."

Alex and I continued past them and looked over the photos taped to boards held up by easels all around the inside of the room.

I felt strange sorrow for the loss of someone I hardly knew. Maybe it was because I was the last person waiting for her, wondering why she hadn't shown up.

I gazed at a photo of Sarah holding a young boy I was sure was Wyatt. There were photos of Jeffrey and Sarah. I'd only noticed a single photograph of Melinda and Sarah together. But it was obvious they were sisters. They looked a lot alike, something I didn't realize until then, since I never had the chance to meet Sarah.

I felt a hand on my arm and turned to Alex, next to me, but her eyes were on the photos. It was Melinda.

She stood behind us, and without a second thought I gave her a hug. She held onto me for a few moments, then turned to Alex. "Thank you for coming," she said with her back to Jeffrey and Wyatt.

I looked past her and saw Jeffrey with his eyes on us. But he turned away as soon as I caught his eye.

· · · · ● · ● · · · ·

The Jenner's house was in San Marco on the west side of River Road. I walked in and my eyes went across the wide-open interior toward the back side of the house. It was an entire wall made of glass. And off in the distance past their lush, green lawn was the St. Johns.

I leaned toward Alex with my voice lowered. "I thought *I* had the best view, living on the boat." My eyes shifted from the view through the glass to the crowd of people who had gathered in the Jenner's home. "I guess architects do all right?"

From behind us I heard a familiar voice. "Henry?"

I turned and Chloe and Jake were there, standing behind us.

Before anyone said a word I pulled them both through a doorway and into an empty room. I didn't close the door, but looked behind me to make sure nobody else had followed. "Listen, nobody needs to know who I am or why I'm here. We're friends of Sarah's...if anyone asks. There's nothing more to it."

Jake nodded. "I know. I haven't said a word to anyone."

I gave Jake a nod then turned my eyes to Chloe. "You don't know anything about us. Anyone asks, you barely know my name." I gave them both a quick nod. "You cool?"

Both Jake and Chloe nodded back.

Jake said, "Who are you, again?" He smiled.

"Perfect," I said.

As we all turned to leave the room, Wyatt Jenner stopped and stood in front of us in the doorway. "Is everything all right?"

"Hey, Wyatt," Jake said. Chloe reached out her arms and gave Wyatt a hug. "Are you doing all right?"

He nodded, but with little expression on his face. "Thanks for coming."

I said, "Hi Wyatt. We met earlier."

He nodded. "Yeah, I know. My dad asked me if I knew who you were." He looked at the four of us. "You all know each other?"

Jake looked right at me, clearly caught off guard. He turned to Wyatt. "They come in the restaurant." Jake glanced at me, then turned to Alex. "I'm sorry, you said your names are Henry and Alex, right?"

Alex and I exchanged a quick look and played along with Jake. He tried a little too hard.

I put my arm over Alex's shoulder and tried to leave the room.

Chloe said, "We'll talk to you in a little bit." She grabbed Jake by the arm. They both stepped past Wyatt and back out to the main area of the house.

Wyatt stepped in front of the doorway, although I wasn't sure if it was intentional or not. He looked back and forth from me to Alex. "So did you know my mom from work?"

I nodded. "You could say that." I looked past him, through the doorway and into the crowd.

Wyatt, Alex and I stood in silence for a moment. Wyatt looked around the room, filled with nice furniture. It looked like a showroom at a store. "Mom used to call this the *living room*. But we never spent much time in here, with all this fancy furniture. I never understood why you'd call a room a *'living room'* if you never really get to live in it."

Neither of us responded but Wyatt turned and started through the doorway. "I should head out there," he said. "I've been told I have to mingle with the guests."

We walked out after him and moved toward the back of the house, to what almost felt like you were outside, with the entire wall made of glass. The Jenner's home had become filled with dozens of guests, at the least.

I leaned into Alex. "I don't expect half this crowd when I die." I shrugged. "Might just be you and Billy, assuming you don't have anything better to do. I guess my parents would come, if they're still around." I looked through the glass wall toward the river. "And who would host a party like this?" I rubbed my chin. "Maybe have it at the marina?"

Alex rolled her eyes and walked away from me.

I looked outside again and spotted Melinda out on the patio. She was with an older gentleman with white hair slicked back on his pinkish scalp. Their discussion looked to be somewhat animated, but it was hard to tell.

Alex walked up behind me and tapped my arm then handed me a drink. "Here. I think you need this."

I took the glass from her hand. I looked over the rim and took a sip of whiskey. My eyes were on Melinda and the old man.

Alex sipped her glass of wine and looked outside. "Did you talk to Melinda?"

Before I could answer, Jeffrey came up behind us. He gave Alex a nod and shifted his eyes back to mine. "You said your name was Henry Walsh, is that right?" He turned back to Alex and pointed a finger at her and sipped from a martini glass. "Alex Jepson, right?" He stared at her over the rim of his glass.

Alex gave him a nod.

He said, "Is that short for something? Alexandria, perhaps?"

"Yes, Alexandria."

He looked her up and down, as if I wasn't even there. "That's a pretty name," he said, then turned back to me. "I know you're both private investigators."

Alex and I exchanged a look, but neither of us gave him an answer.

I looked past him for a moment, when my eyes noticed a stain on the ceiling.

Jeffrey turned and followed my eyes. "Are you here to investigate the plumbing?" He laughed. "We've had a leak...I finally got it fixed." He looked back at me with a nod. "You must be very good at whatever it is you do." He shrugged. "I guess I should've called the painters before we had guests at the house."

Alex and I still hadn't said much at all. It didn't take me long to realize I didn't like the guy at all.

Jeffrey looked off for a moment then took a step closer to us both. "Did Sarah hire you to keep an eye on me?"

I hesitated a moment then shook my head. "Excuse me?" I played dumb, although the truth was that she *hadn't* ever actually hired us. She never got the chance.

A waitress dressed in a tuxedo and bowtie came toward us and asked if we'd like a drink. Jeffrey threw his head back and finished the martini in his hand. He put the glass on her tray and shook his head. "No, my two guests were just getting ready to leave." The waitress walked away and he turned to us, his arms folded at his chest. He narrowed his eyes. "Do I look like a fool?"

I looked back at him but I wasn't sure how to answer. "You mean because of those glasses that don't seem to fit your face?"

He ignored my comment. "Next time I walk by here you had better be gone, or I'll have someone from the sheriff's office over to escort you out." He kept his eyes on me for a moment. "I'd rather not have to do that in front of Sarah's friends."

He turned and walked off into the crowd.

Alex gave me a look. "I think we should go."

I hesitated and looked through the glass toward the patio. "I wanted to ask who that old man is, out there with Melinda."

Jake and Chloe walked up to us. I nodded through the glass. "Do me a favor, see if you can find out who that older gentleman is out there. We have to leave. It seems we've worn out our welcome."

Without another word I reached for Alex's hand, pulled her through the crowd and headed out the door.

Chapter 5

I PULLED INTO THE marina and my phone buzzed. I parked a few spaces down from my boat then looked at my phone, read a text from Jake. He'd sent me a picture of the man who was talking to Melinda at the Jenner's house when we left.

The text included with the image read:

The man's name is Mickey Hendrick

Alex and I stepped out of the Jeep. We walked toward my boat and I showed her the photo. "Jake just sent a picture of that older guy with Melinda at the Jepson's house. Name's Mickey Hendrick."

Alex stepped ahead of me and I helped her up onto the boat. She sat down on one of the bow seats while I stepped down below to change out of my fancy clothes and get into something more comfortable.

I threw the suit coat on top of my unmade bed with the pile of laundry I'd left from three days before. I unbuttoned my shirt and pulled off my pants, draped them over a chair in the galley then grabbed a pair of shorts and a t-shirt from the same chair.

I turned toward the ladder and Alex's long legs were coming down. I looked away and said, "What are you doing down here?" I was embarrassed by the mess. Although it was nothing she hadn't seen before.

She put both feet down on the floor and looked around with her hands on her hips. "Wow, this is quite the mess."

I put my hand on her back and pushed her toward the ladder. "Come on, I told you to wait up top. You don't need to be down here."

She laughed and grabbed onto the ladder and started up top.

With my eyes down to the floor, I waited for her to make it all the way up before I looked up and followed behind her.

Alex stood and watched me come up onto the deck. She said, "Did you notice any young, attractive women there?"

I shrugged. "Actually, I noticed a few attractive women."

Alex gave me a look. "Is that what you do at a service when someone's died? Check out the women?"

I shrugged. "Didn't you just ask me if..."

"I meant Emma, the young woman from Jeffrey's firm."

We both climbed down off the boat and headed for the Jeep.

My phone rang in my pocket. "It's Melinda."

I answered, and right away she said, "Where'd you go? I thought you said you'd be at Sarah's?"

"We were there," I said. "But Jeffrey asked us to leave."

"He *what*? Why? He didn't know who you were, did he?"

"He did. He knew exactly who we were. I don't know if he knew before we saw him at the service, or if he asked around when he saw us at his house. But he came right out and admitted he knew Sarah had hired us."

I climbed up into the Jeep, the phone in my ear.

Melinda said, "So what'd you tell him?"

"That he was wrong. She never hired us. And that's not even a lie, technically."

"Well, you missed quite the scene," she said. "A friend of Sarah's got into a screaming match with Emma, the young woman from Jeffrey's office. She called her out in front of all the guests, came right out and told her she should be ashamed for showing up when everyone knew she was sleeping with Jeffrey."

"That must not have gone over very well," I said. "What'd Jeffrey do?"

"Threw her out. The party was over after that."

"What about Wyatt? Was he there for it?"

She said, "He left as soon as she started yelling. I'm not sure where he went."

I put the hand over the phone and said to Alex, "Emma Buckman was there. Must have showed up after we left. One of Sarah's friends got into it with her." I put the phone back up to my ear. "Who was the friend?"

"Her name's Kelly Swift. She's a good friend of Sarah's. They worked together at Hendrick Logistics."

I said, "Isn't that the woman Sarah was supposed to meet before she met me?"

"Yes. Kelly and Sarah used to work out together every morning before work. She was the last person to hear from Sarah. It was a text, actually."

I said, "Who was the guy you were talking to outside the house?"

"You were watching me?" she said. "And you didn't come out?"

"Like I said, I was dealing with Jeffrey. But I saw you with some guy. He had white hair. He was older, but maybe not as old as he looked."

She was quiet on the other end for a brief moment. "That was Sarah's boss, Mickey Hendrick. He owns Hendrick Logistics."

I said, "Well, I noticed your conversation looked a bit animated. I wasn't sure if—"

"Animated? I don't think so. He was quite upset. He really liked Sarah."

"Do you know him pretty well?"

"Not really," she said. "Sarah used to talk about him all the time. I think they had a pretty good working relationship."

· · · · ● · ● · · · ·

I sat in the darkness outside in the street and watched Jeffrey's house. I needed concrete evidence that Jeffrey had even the slightest motive for killing his wife.

Emma was very young. Especially for a man in his forties. She was in fact what Alex called a *digital native*. Meaning she was born into the digital world. She was also very digitally social compared to those of us born at a time when everything in your life wasn't shared with the world. With just a few clicks, we knew where she worked, who her friends were, and what she did for fun. It was all there, out in the open for anybody to see.

The garage door opened at Jeffrey Jenner's house. An engine roared when he backed his red convertible Corvette onto the driveway. He whipped it around and took off with his tires spinning. He turned from the driveway toward North River Road.

He drove right past the Jeep without a clue it was me. But he drove fast and was far ahead.

It was hard for me to keep up in a Jeep built for going off-road. Never mind being in pursuit of a car that'd go well into the hundreds.

I kept my eyes ahead and Jeffrey took a quick right onto LaSalle, then crossed San Marco Boulevard and cut up Belmonte.

Jeffrey's Corvette moved fast. He weaved it in-and-out of traffic and I did all I could to keep up. His brakes lit-up when he stopped in front of what I remembered to be the historic South Jacksonville Grammar School. But it was no longer a school, and had been converted into what was called the Lofts of San Marco, a trendy apartment building right in the heart of San Marco.

It didn't take long to figure out what Jeffrey was doing there. Because as soon as he stepped from his car, a very attractive young woman I'd recognized from the dozens of photos online ran from the front door of the building and jumped into his arms.

Emma and Jeffrey embraced each other and kissed right there on the sidewalk in front of the apartments.

For a man who had just buried his wife hours before...he seemed to be holding up okay. And didn't seem to care whether or not anybody saw him.

I stayed clear from their view and took as many photos as I could until she pulled him by the hand into the building.

I dialed my phone and called Alex. "This was too easy," I said. I looked up at the building. "I'm outside a place called the Lofts of San Marco. It's the old South Jacksonville Grammar School...which is fitting since Jeffrey was just standing out in plain sight, making out with a girl who looked like she just got out of grammar school."

"What a low life," Alex said. "The night of his own wife's service? I don't care how rocky their marriage may have been..."

"Part of me wanted him to see me. Just so he'd know we had him." I looked along the building. "What about you? Any luck with the sheriff's office?"

"Can you meet?" she said. "You'll want to see this."

· · · · ● · ● · · · ·

Alex sat at the bar at Billy's Place and turned just as I came up behind her.

"Where's Billy?" I said.

Chloe walked out from the back kitchen and delivered two plates to an older couple seated down the other end of the bar. She replaced their empty wine glasses with full glasses of red, then turned and walked toward us. "I was wondering where you went earlier."

"You mean at the Jenner's?"

Chloe nodded and put a glass with two rocks down in front of me. She poured me a healthy double-shot of Jack. "Mr. Jenner asked us about you."

"I figured he would," I said. "What'd you say?"

She shrugged. "Just that I knew you from the restaurant where Jake and I worked. But that was it. I said I didn't know much about you."

"Did he buy it?"

Chloe cracked half a smile and shrugged. "It wasn't a total lie." She turned and walked back into the kitchen.

I turned at Alex. "*What* wasn't a total lie?"

Alex sipped her drink. "I'm guessing the part about Chloe not knowing much about you. Maybe she just meant...between your space bubble and your skillful deflection of any questions about your personal life? She's not that far off the mark."

I sipped my Jack.

Chloe walked out of the kitchen again with a plate in her hand and placed it down in front of Alex.

I looked at my watch. "Late dinner?"

She nodded and turned in her seat. She reached into her backpack on the backrest of her stool and pulled out a folder. "Here," she said and handed it to me.

"Is this the report?"

"Yes. And if I'm being honest, I don't see any indication this was anything more than a bad car accident. In fact, there'd been five similar incidents in the past year on that same corner."

"Five? But did anybody else die?"

Alex had already leaned over her plate and took a bite of her dinner. She finished what was in her mouth and held up her index finger. She wiped her mouth and shook her head. "Sarah's was the only death."

Chapter 6

I MET MELINDA AT Friendship Fountain and brought her a coffee, assuming she'd appreciate the gesture.

I assumed wrong.

She appeared to smile then she shook her head. "Thank you, but I don't drink coffee."

I sat down next to her on the bench with a cup of coffee in each hand.

I leaned over and placed one down on the ground next to my foot. "I followed Jeffrey last night. And he doesn't seem to care about hiding his relationship with Emma."

"You saw them together?"

"Yes, I followed him to her apartment. She lives at the Lofts of San Marco."

She turned to me. "I used to live there."

"No kidding?" I said, "Well that's where he was last night."

She slowly shook her head. "The night of Sarah's service and..." She closed her eyes. "The man is unbelievable."

I sipped my coffee and handed her the folder I had tucked under my arm. "Here are some photos."

She opened the envelope, pulled out the photos and slid them back in without taking much of a look. "I don't need to see them. Not right now."

I took the folder and put it down on the bench between us. "I had a look at the accident report."

Melinda watched me, waiting.

I stared straight ahead. "That road where Sara had her accident...it's a dangerous turn. There've already been five accidents in the past year, right at that same spot."

"Five?"

"Yes. But Sarah's was the only fatality."

Her eyes seemed to go well past the fountain, out toward the St. Johns. Without turning to me, she said, "I'm not paying you to tell me what's already been in the paper, or what the police believe is the truth, just because some patrolmen were in a hurry to finish their paperwork."

"It sounds like you already have something against the cops." I watched her eyes, still out somewhere else. "I know plenty of good men and women in law enforcement."

She looked at me, her eyes narrowed. "Don't try to convince me that cops are perfect."

"That's not what I'm doing, Melinda. But the sheriff's office investigated your sister's accident. Even if Jeffrey was cheating on your sister—and it appears he was—it still doesn't mean he caused her accident. Or that *anybody* caused her accident."

She closed her eyes and folded her arms at her chest. "So is that it? You're so sure my sister's death was an accident, you're going to tell me I shouldn't question anything? Why, because of what someone else told you?" She wouldn't look at me. "I heard you were a man who would do anything to get to the truth. I know that's why Sarah called you in the first place." She got up from the bench and walked away. It was like we were playing the same game like the night she was at my office.

I grabbed the folder from the bench and bent down to pick up the second cup of coffee. I followed after her. "Melinda, wait. Take this."

She stopped and turned to me and I reached into my back pocket. I pulled out a small envelope I'd folded in half and handed it to her. "Here, this is yours."

She tilted her head. "What's this?"

"Your deposit."

"Are you serious?"

"I'm not going to charge you for the work I did. But I don't think there's anything else I can do."

"Wow," she said. She walked away without taking the envelope from my hand. "I'll have to do a better job checking references next time."

I stood and watched her. "Melinda, wait. I want you to take this. Please."

She continued toward the San Marco Boulevard circle and disappeared beyond the cars.

My phone vibrated in my pocket.

It was Alex. "Where are you?" she said.

"Friendship Fountain. What about you?"

"I was going to come by your boat. I thought you'd be there."

"Give me twenty minutes, I'm on my way. Why?"

"I found something I need to show you about the accident."

"Oh, well...I sort of just told Melinda we weren't going to take the case."

"You *what*? Why?"

I knew I should have discussed it a little more with Alex, but still had trouble forgetting it wasn't *only* my business anymore. "Well, between the police report and, well...I don't know. Jeffrey doesn't seem to have much to hide. I don't think he cares who knows he's with Emma." I looked at the smaller of the two envelopes in my hand. "But she wouldn't take the deposit back."

"Okay, well, you know what you have to do?"

I walked toward my Jeep. "I think you're going to tell me."

"Call her back and tell her you were wrong."

· · · · · ● · ● · · · ·

I was up on my boat with a glass of Jack Daniels. I saw Alex in her yellow Jeep out on Trout River Road, and watched her turn into the marina parking lot. She parked a few spaces down from my boat and stepped out with something in her hand. I didn't know what it was.

She cocked her head a bit and gave me a look. "You're drinking?"

I looked at my glass from the side and nodded. "Something wrong with that?"

She looked at her watch. "It's ten in the morning."

I took a sip of my drink and leaned back against my boat.

Alex sighed and shook her head. "Why'd you tell Melinda we weren't going to take the case...after we promised her we would? And—I know you know this, but—we'd already agreed to make these decisions together."

I looked down toward the dock before shifting my eyes to Alex. "I wanted to help her. She was just so sure...like she knew what happened, but wanted us to prove her theory. I was, I don't know... I just don't see how we'd be able to give her what she was looking for. Which, to me, was to nail Jeffrey Jenner. No matter what."

Alex paused and stared back at me. She pushed her hair back from her face with the wind blowing at her back. "You don't look like you're happy about any of this," she said. There was a look of concern on her face.

I took another sip of Jack and wanted to jump back on the boat for a refill. But thought I'd hold off for a bit. "I wanted to help her. But..." I looked Alex in the eye. "I'm sorry I made the call without you."

She held her eyes on mine for a couple of moments then handed me the papers in her hand.

"What's this?" I said. I scanned over the first page. I held up my empty glass. "You want a drink?"

Alex paused before answering. "Is this what you're going to do? Sit on the dock and drink all day?"

I shrugged. "Thinking about it."

Alex shook her head. With her hands on her hips, she turned and faced the water. "You walked away from a client without discussing it with me, now you're going to drink your bad decision away?"

I said, "I thought we agreed there wasn't much to it."

"But I thought we had more work to do before we decided. And I never suggested we should turn our back on the only client we've had in two months."

I looked down at the dock. "Melinda seems to be a very emotional woman."

Alex stared at me for a moment, crossing her arms. "Do you want to tell me what that's supposed to mean?"

I hesitated, knowing I wasn't going to get my point across. Mainly because I knew I didn't have one.

"So now what?" I said. "We know the husband wasn't faithful. It sounds like Sarah wasn't any better."

Alex kept her eyes on me for a couple of moments. "You're not feeling anything?"

I held up my empty glass. "From this?"

Alex rolled her eyes and shook her head. "No, I mean. In your gut? Even in the past when we've had nothing to go by, something in your gut has always told you to stick with it. But now... You honestly don't think there's anything to this?" She seemed to ease up on me a bit. "Because if you don't, then..."

"Then what?" I said.

"I don't know. Maybe you're right. But, it's..." She went quiet for a moment. "You've had bullets flying past your head and you didn't turn your back on a case."

I stepped toward the edge of the dock and looked out toward the water. "I can tell her I changed my mind, if that's what you want me to do?" I reached up onto my head, surprised to feel my sunglasses and pulled them down over my eyes. "Oh, look at that. I was looking for these..."

Alex grabbed the empty glass from my hand. "I think you've had enough to drink. Maybe we can grab a coffee, then swing by the scene."

"The scene? You mean where Sarah's car went off the road?"

Alex nodded. "Don't you think that would be the smart thing to do?"

I scratched my head. "Why haven't we done that yet?"

Alex shook her head, stared at me with a look of disappointment on her face. "Because for some reason, for the first time since I've known you, you actually believe the cops got it right."

Chapter 7

ALEX AND I STOOD on just off the road and looked down toward the creek at the bottom of the embankment. Sarah had sustained head and neck injuries from the crash, but the cause of death was by drowning.

She was found facedown in the water, just outside her car.

You could see the clearing through the vegetation and brush where the car had clearly traveled before hitting the water.

I sipped my coffee from the paper cup. "Do you know how deep that creek is?"

Alex shaded her eyes and turned to me. "Her body was barely under the water. But I'd bet it's three or four feet in the middle."

I turned and looked back at the road coming toward us. It disappeared around the sharp turn where Sarah—and others before her—had taken the same path into the creek.

Alex started along the road and walked toward the large live oak on the corner. "Report says Sarah likely pulled the wheel at the last second to avoid that tree. But in doing so, she lost control and took her car down the embankment."

There were no cars on the road. There was almost no sound other than the birds and tree frogs and cicadas.

I looked down the embankment again with my back to the road. I yelled to Alex, over near the tree almost thirty yards away. "It's a sharp turn. But you'd have to be distracted or not paying attention... Driving at a pretty good clip."

Alex walked toward me. "She sent a text to Kelly Swift that morning, told her she was going to take her own car to the gym."

"What time?"

Alex said, "They suspect the accident was between five and seven, but they haven't been able to narrow it down anymore than that. Kelly normally picked her up at five-thirty, they'd drive to the gym together for a six o'clock class."

I lifted my sunglasses from my eyes. "They worked out together every morning?"

Alex walked past me, heading down the embankment. "Sarah sent the text to Kelly at five in the morning."

I followed Alex and walked along the tire tracks that had cut through the grass and vegetation. Hard rain had fallen in the area overnight, so it made it hard to get a clear picture. I crouched down and touched the muddy ground. "What were the conditions that morning? Did it rain?"

Alex nodded and continued down to the edge of the creek.

I stopped and looked up at the road, following the tracks with my eyes to the top of the embankment. Being careful not to lose my footing, I walked back up to the road.

Alex was at the bottom, near the water. "Where are you going?"

I didn't answer right away, turned from the road and from the top, tracing the tracks with my gaze on the creek. I looked back and forth from the sharp turn with the live oak and assumed the path from the road. But the tracks seemed to go straight down to the creek. I said to Alex. "I understand the car was likely out of control, but you look at the way those tires hit the edge of the road, it's as if she drove straight from across the road."

Alex climbed back up top and stood in front of me, her foot up on the edge of the embankment. "What are you saying?"

I pointed toward the sharp turn, held my arm straight toward the live oak. I stared, as if looking through the site of a gun, one eye closed. "The path from the road and the one her car took doesn't jive. She would've had to cut the wheel right there." I pointed toward the road in front of us. "Looking at this track, it's almost a ninety-degree turn."

Alex looked back toward the creek. "Well, like it says in the report, her car was likely out of control. I'm not sure the angle of her car, in this case, tells us much."

I pointed toward a line of trees along the road, a few feet from where we stood. "She'd have to have gone all the way to the other side of this road. And I can't see how she'd miss those trees." I turned back to Alex. "The other accidents...did they all end up down in the creek?"

Alex shook her head. "No. Only one of them. She nodded toward a tree with bark that'd clearly been damaged at one time, but new bark had grown. The tree had started to repair itself. She said, "I believe the driver hit this tree, first."

I looked back and forth from the road to the creek. "Maybe the wet roads changed the car's trajectory, but I don't see how she'd get the car down into that creek without first flipping her vehicle if she cuts the wheel that hard."

Alex shifted her eyes from me then back and forth along the road. She stared down at the tracks on the embankment.

I kneeled down. "These tracks are almost too clean. They're too straight. I wouldn't say it indicates a driver who was out of control." I climbed further down the embankment and touched the bark on the tree Alex had pointed to. I looked up toward the road. "How could she miss this tree?" I shook my head. "Are you sure the sheriff's office actually came out here to the scene?"

Alex came down behind me and walked past me toward the creek. She looked back at me as I pulled out my phone. "Who are you calling?"

"Melinda," I said. "I need to apologize." I listened for the ring. "Then I'll tell her we're going to investigate this case, whether she wants us to or not."

············

I stood outside the tall office building and watched Melinda walk out through a revolving glass door. She had what looked like a kid's lunch bag in one hand, a Thermos in the other.

She didn't give me much of a greeting. "I don't have much time, and need to eat my lunch." She looked up toward the blue sky. "I don't want to spend such a nice day eating at my desk."

We sat down together at a table in the middle of a small park just outside her building, where dozens of other worker bees walked past us. Some carried bags almost identical to the one Melinda carried, and searched for open seats at the other tables around us.

There was a sign up on a metal post that read, *Private Property. P.A.S. Employees Only.*

I nodded toward the sign. "Am I going to get in trouble for being here?"

Melinda cracked a slight smile and pulled a cup of yogurt from her bag. "I'll tell them I know you." She had her eyes down and removed the aluminum from the top of her yogurt. She stuck a stainless steel spoon inside and looked up at me. "Are you going to tell me why you're here?"

I didn't hesitate a moment. "To say I'm sorry."

She stared straight into my eyes, then again down into her yogurt. She stuck a spoonful in her mouth, turned the spoon and pulled it from her lips upside down. "I don't expect you to apologize," she said. "I understand, you run a business. You can't waste your time on—"

"No, I was wrong. I'm sorry for that. I should have listened. I'm sorry I didn't dig into what happened a little deeper."

She stared back at me but didn't respond to what I'd said. Her eyes went past me. "Although you weren't wrong to suggest I might be letting my emotions get in the way of the truth. I just wanted to blame Jeffrey for Sarah's death. I guess...it was just wishful thinking." She looked up at me. "He's still a piece of—"

"Didn't you listen to my message?" I said.

"I did. Most of it, I think." She shrugged. "You said you'd be here at noon. Was there more?"

I rubbed my face and nodded. "Oh, okay. That explains it...what I said was although I can't tell you for sure who is responsible for what happened, Alex and I both agree the so-called accident looks suspicious."

"Suspicious? In what way?"

"It's hard to say for sure. There's been a lot of rain and too much time has passed. The evidence at the scene is likely compromised. But we believe there's a good chance her accident was staged. Again, we could be wrong. But it just doesn't look like she could've gone down that embankment the way she was driving on that road."

Melinda closed her eyes and lowered her head. She placed her cup of yogurt on the table. When she looked up at me, she had tears in her eyes. "So, does that mean you'll let me hire you?"

I shook my head and put the envelope with her original deposit down in front of her. "We'll help you. But there's not going to be a fee. We'll call it *pro bono*.

Chapter 8

Alex and I stepped from the Jeep and walked toward Kelly Swift. She had her back to us with a garden hose in her hand and appeared to have headphones over her ears, bopping her head back and forth. She clearly didn't notice us approaching.

But I should've known better when I walked up behind her and tapped on her shoulder. She turned, startled, and shot a stream of water at my chest like it was a gun.

She ripped the earphones from her ears and backed up a step, the hose still pointed at me.

"Sorry," I said with my hands up. "I'm Henry Walsh." With a tip of my head to the side, I introduced Alex. "This is my partner, Alex Jepson."

She held the nozzle of the hose toward me, like it was a gun. "Partner?"

I nodded. "We're private investigators."

She stared for a moment before she turned and walked toward the house to where the hose was connected and turned the spigot. She hung the nozzle on a nail and wiped her hands on her shorts.

Kelly was medium build and pretty, with her strawberry-blonde hair tied up on her head. Her arms were tight with muscle and she wore a white-t-shirt a size or two too big. I didn't notice a ring on her finger when she adjusted her wet t-shirt.

"So, why are there two private investigators on my lawn this morning?"

I looked toward the BMW in the driveway of the L-shaped ranch made of brick. From what it looked like, Kelly appeared to do all right for herself.

I said, "We'd like to ask you some questions, if you have a few minutes?"

She shrugged. "What about?"

"Sarah Jenner."

The expression on her face changed. Her eyes went down to the grass and she put both hands on her hips, tapping the ground with the front of her bare foot. "I suppose I..." She didn't finish, her eyes locked on mine for a moment. "Who hired you?"

Alex put her hands on her hips and shifted her stance. "We're investigating the accident. Pretty standard stuff, just so we can confirm some information."

"Who did you say you were with?" She looked back and forth from me to Alex. "The sheriff's office?" She brushed a strand of hair from her face and pushed it back on her head.

I handed her my business card. "We're independent." I looked around the yard. "Do you have somewhere we can talk for a few minutes?"

Kelly gestured toward the corner of the house. "We can go in the back and sit down." She started ahead of us, but stopped and turned. "Can I offer either of you a drink?"

We both declined.

As we turned the corner behind her, Kelly continued walking but turned to us over her shoulder. "So is there something wrong? I mean, with the accident? I haven't heard anything from the sheriff's office."

"But you did speak with them?" I said.

She nodded. "Yes, of course. She was supposed to meet me at the gym. Normally we'd drive together, but..." She turned her eyes away from us. "Every single day we'd go together. Usually I'd drive. But for some reason, she decided to meet me."

Alex's eyes shot wide open. "You work out seven days a week?"

Kelly smiled and shook her head. "No, not on weekends. But it's how we'd start our day. I'd pick her up at five-thirty for a six o'clock class." She looked around her yard. "On weekends, I get my workout outside, in the yard. It's therapeutic." She looked up at the sky and squinted her eyes. "Especially when it's such a beautiful day like today."

"You must feel pretty lucky," I said.

We sat down at a round, glass table on the stone patio just outside the french doors at the back of her house.

"Lucky?' She shook her head with a somewhat confused look on her face.

"Well, I guess, lucky you weren't in the car with her. If normally you'd be in the same car together?"

Kelly said, "But maybe it wouldn't have happened if she'd driven with me." She closed her eyes for a moment and put her head down in her hand. "It's just such a tragedy. I don't know why she decided to drive alone."

Alex and I exchanged a look. Something didn't feel right.

"Didn't you tell the sheriff's office you were the one who decided to go to the gym earlier than normal?"

"Oh, well...no. That's not true. What I told them was Sarah and I had talked the night before. I had decided to go in earlier than normal. I've had a pain in my back and I thought I'd do some back work before our class."

I said, "So you told her to drive alone?"

"I was going to pick her up at five. But she sent me a text, saying she'd just meet me there at the normal time." She stood up from the table. Her gaze shifted between me and Alex. "Would you like a drink?"

We both shook our heads Kelly walked toward the house.

"We should ask to see the text," Alex said, her voice hushed.

But before I could answer Kelly had come back through the french doors. She walked toward us with a glass in her hand and sat down next to me, across from Alex. "If you change your mind and want a drink, please don't hesitate to ask." She sipped her drink then held the glass with both hands down on the table. Her eyes were down on the table. "It's just so hard to believe she's gone."

Alex shifted in her chair and leaned forward. "You and Sarah were very close, is that right?"

Kelly said, "She was one of my closest friends."

I backed my chair away from the table and turned so I could look straight at Kelly. "We heard what happened at Jeffrey's house."

Kelly scratched behind her ear and again looked down into her glass. "I'm sorry that happened. I had too much to drink. But I was just so mad. It was supposed to be the time to celebrate Sarah's life. And that whore shows up..."

"What made you so sure about her?"

"About who?"

"Emma Buckman. How did you know Jeffrey was having an affair with her? Because, the truth is, Sarah was going to hire us to follow him. But as far as we know, she didn't have any proof he was actually having an affair."

Kelly seemed to swallow hard and looked away. She took her time before she spoke. "I know Emma. Not well, but we've had some interactions through work, from when the new Hendrick Logistics building was built. I knew she worked with Jeffrey. Sarah was never sure." She nodded. "You're right, she had no proof. But I was sure of it. Sure enough, anyway." She scratched the side of her head. "But she never said anything to me about hiring a private investigator to follow him." She took a sip from her glass and stood from her seat. "Excuse me for a moment." Without another word, she walked back toward her house and disappeared through the french doors.

I looked toward the house and waited a moment before I turned to Alex. "If they had discussed Jeffrey's affair, why wouldn't Kelly have known about Sarah wanting to hire us?"

Alex's eyes shifted toward the house then back to mine. "She's not acting like someone who has nothing to hide, the way she keeps going in the house."

Kelly walked out through the doors and back toward us. She sat down next to me. "Sorry about that, I had to check on something in the wash."

I watched her shift in her seat. Her eyes moved around the yard. It was clear she didn't want to look at me or Alex.

Alex said, "So how did you and Sarah meet?"

Kelly put on a slight, yet forced smile. "We worked together. I was actually the one who hired her."

"So you were her boss?"

Kelly shook her head. "No. But when she decided to get back to work after Wyatt left for school, I convinced Mickey to hire her."

"Mickey Hendrick?" I said.

She nodded. "Oh yes. Sorry. Mickey Hendrick. Sarah was smart and very bright. She had already been a CFO with another company, prior to having Wyatt. But it's not ever easy getting back into the workplace after you've left to raise a child. Mickey and I both liked her right away, as soon as we met in her interviews."

"You said you convinced *them*?" I said. "Is there someone else besides Mickey Hendrick who gets involved in who gets hired?"

"Oh well, yes. Of course. It's a boy's club upstairs." She smiled and glanced at Alex. "You must know what I mean?"

Alex shrugged and shook her head but didn't really answer.

I said, "So you and Sarah became friends *after* she was hired?"

She nodded. "We got along very well, from day one. We were both very driven. I guess the only difference is I never left to have kids."

"Is there a Mister Swift?" Alex said.

Kelly shook her head. "I was married for a short time. But that's another story." She reached in her pocket and pulled out her phone. "Oh my, look at that." She turned her eyes to mine. "I'm sorry, but I have to get ready...I have somewhere I need to be."

Alex and I stood from the table. "Not a problem," I said. "I appreciate your time."

Kelly led us around toward the front of the house but stood by the gate.

Alex and I walked to the Jeep and when I turned to look back, she was gone.

Chapter 9

Mickey Hendrick was in a meeting when Alex and I arrived at the Hendrick Logistics offices just off East Adams Street.

The old woman behind the desk in the reception area barely made eye contact with us. "Mr. Hendrick doesn't normally have visitors without an appointment."

I said, "I understand he's a busy man. But, maybe if you tell him there's someone here to talk about Sarah Jenner, he'll make an exception?" I gave the woman behind the desk a tight smile. "And you can say I promise it won't take long."

The woman looked up and kept her gaze on me for a moment before she reached for the phone and put it up to her ear. After a few moments she put it down. "I'm sorry, but he's not answering. As I said, he's likely still in his meeting."

"Doesn't he have an assistant or someone we can talk to? Make sure we get to see him as soon as he's done?"

The woman paused and looked up at me from behind her desk. "That's who I called. She's most likely in the meeting with him." She handed me a piece of paper. "This is her direct line. Call her, tell her what it's about and you need to see him right away."

Alex and I sat in the chair along the wall and I looked down at the paper. "I'll give her a call. But I think we'll wait right here."

Before the woman could say a word, the double glass doors to the side of the reception area swung open. Right away I recognized Mickey Hendrick, surrounded by four other men, all five dressed in the same dark suits and laughed out loud. They walked right past us, as if we weren't there.

Mickey stopped at the door and shook each man's hand. He slapped the last one on the back as the man walked out the door. Mickey turned when the men were out of sight and the big smile was gone from his face. He shook his head and under his breath said, "Cheap sons of bitches...want everything for free." He hadn't noticed me and Alex in the chairs behind him.

The woman behind the desk spoke up. "Uh, excuse me, Mr. Hendrick?" She nodded toward me and Alex. "There's someone here to see you about Sarah."

Mickey was on the short side with a thick body and a belly that hung over his belt. He had a receding hairline with white hair, slicked back on his pink scalp.

Alex and I stood from our chairs when he turned from the door. He put on the same big smile he wore a moment ago. But he stared back at me and the smile ran away from his face. "This is about Sarah?" His eyes were on me at first, but quickly shifted to Alex. He looked her up and down then shifted his eyes back to me. "Who are you?"

"Henry Walsh." He gave me a quick handshake then extended his hand to Alex. "Mickey Hendrick." He shook her hand but didn't let go right away.

Alex introduced herself and pulled her hand back from his grasp.

I handed him my business card. "We'd like to ask you some questions about Sarah Jenner, if you have a few minutes?"

He reached into his shirt pocket, pulled out a pair of glasses and slipped them on. He looked down at my card. "Private investigators? For what?" His mouth formed a small circle and his eyes shifted back and forth over his glasses.

"If you have some time," I said, "I'll tell you why we're here."

He pulled off his glasses and stuck them in his shirt pocket. "How about *first* you tell me why you're here. Then I'll tell you whether or not I have time?"

Alex and I exchanged a look.

I said, "As I already said, we have questions about Sarah."

"I heard that part," he said. "But what about?"

I didn't answer him and folded my arms at my chest. "Is there somewhere we can talk, in private?"

His face dropped whatever expression he had. He nodded, then turned to the woman behind the desk. "Hold my calls." He looked at his watch then turned back to me. "I don't have a lot of time."

We followed him through the glass doors and down the hall. He turned into an office, closed the door and gestured for me and Alex to sit down in the two chairs in front of his desk. "Would either of you like a coffee?" He pulled open the door. "Maryann, would you bring us some coffee?"

He closed the door and sat down behind his desk. "So, tell me, why would a private investigator be here asking questions about Sarah's accident?"

I leaned forward in the chair. "I didn't say it had to do with her accident."

He stared back at me for a moment. "Then what's it got to do with?"

"We'd just like to know a little about your relationship with Sarah."

He rested his elbows on his desk, his hands folded together in front of his mouth. He shrugged. "I have good relationships with all my employees. We have almost two hundred now." He picked up a gold pen from his desk and leaned back in his chair. "Started this business with nothing, built it up from the ground. If it weren't for the hundred-ninety-seven employees who help keep this ship afloat, I wouldn't be where I am today. This wouldn't be the largest logistics management company in Florida."

There was a knock at the door. It opened and a middle-aged woman with big hips and short legs wrapped in a long, tight dress stepped inside the office. She placed a tray with three mugs and a carafe down on Mr. Hendrick's desk.

Mickey poured coffee into each mug and pushed one in front of Alex and the other toward me. "How do you take it?"

"Black's good for me," I said.

Alex pulled the mug closer and just let it sit there. "This is fine,"

I sipped mine and nodded. "Good coffee." I raised my cup to the woman.

She nodded with a smile and walked out of the office, closing the door behind her.

"So, Mr. Hendrick..."

"Please, call me Mickey."

"I believe you were starting to say you have special relationships with all of your employees? And that Sarah was no different...is that correct?"

He sipped his coffee, his eyes on me from over the rim. "Mind if I call you *Henry*?"

I smiled, my lips tight together. "You can call me whatever you'd like."

He put the mug down and pushed it aside and leaned forward again with his elbows on his desk. "Henry, Sarah was special to me. I'm not going to lie to you. And her death has had a tremendous impact on me. She was a true asset to Hendrick Logistics."

"Was it personal?"

"Was *what* personal?"

"Your relationship with Sarah?"

He looked off for a moment. He squinted a bit, as if he was thinking. Then he shrugged. "As I said, she was an asset to this company. In fact, she was about to be promoted to VP. It was going to be formally announced, until..." He looked down toward the floor.

I glanced at Alex and thought for a moment. "Would that promotion have bothered anyone in your company? As far as I understand, she hadn't been here for very long?"

Mickey reached for his coffee and took another sip. He nodded toward the mug in front of Alex. "You don't like the coffee?"

"It's fine," she said, then grabbed the handle to pull it closer to the edge of the desk. But she didn't take a sip.

"She doesn't drink coffee," I said.

Mickey's eyes opened wide with his eyebrows raised on his head. "You don't drink coffee?" He leaned back in his chair and laughed. "You'd never make it in this place...we go through thousands of dollars in coffee every month. We need it to keep the boys moving."

With a slight tilt to her head, Alex said, "The boys?"

Mickey laughed. "I'm sorry. The employees. Although we *do* have a lot of men working here. It's nothing I ever planned. It might just be the industry. But every once in a while, a smart woman like Sarah comes around, pushes everyone out of her way." He looked down into his mug. "She was something special."

He looked up at me from across the desk and squinted his eyes. "So are you working for the insurance company or something?" He looked back and forth from me to Alex. "It *was* an accident, wasn't it?" I could've been wrong, but it looked like Mickey's eyes had glossed-over.

I wasn't sure if either Mickey was a damn good actor, or he was genuinely and sincerely upset about what had happened to Sarah.

I didn't think I needed to answer his question about why we were there. "You seem to have cared about her. I mean, it seems maybe she was more to you than just another employee?"

He cocked his head back. "What exactly are you trying to imply?"

"I'm not *trying* to imply anything. Like I said, we're just asking questions."

He picked up his mug and took another sip then turned a photo around toward me and Alex. "I've been happily married to the same woman for forty-three years." He paused for a moment. "I'm not saying it's always been perfect, but..."

Alex grabbed the framed photo from the desk and looked at the picture of Mickey's wife. "She's a beautiful woman."

Mickey nodded. "Thank you." He said, "So then, why don't you tell me who hired you?"

Before I could answer, there was a knock at the door. The same woman who had brought us our coffee stuck her head in the door. "Mr. Hendrick, your ride is here."

Chapter 10

I PULLED INTO ALEX's driveway. Her dog Raz barked from inside, his big head in one of the windows with his nose against the glass.

Alex started to step out of the Jeep.

"You have plans tonight?" I said.

She turned to me from outside the passenger side. "I thought I'd research Hendrick Logistics a little further, see what else there is to know about Mickey." She said, "Why?"

I hung my wrist over the steering wheel and glanced toward her house. "I don't know. I wasn't sure if you wanted to grab a bite to eat. Maybe have a drink. Relax a little." I turned to her. "But if you want to work, I get it. It's probably not the worst idea. You've had a long day."

She smiled. "We both have."

We were both quiet for a moment or two.

I said, "You know, it bothers me that I turned my back on someone who wanted our help."

Alex didn't respond right away. "Even if we're able to prove it wasn't an accident, we'll still have a long way to go. And then we'll need to prove the sheriff's office made a mistake."

I thought for a moment. "You know, the more I think about it, there was something about Sarah's call that didn't make sense. I'm not sure I just assumed she wanted to hire us to prove Jeffrey was cheating on her. But..."

Alex grabbed onto the roll bar above her head and stared back at me. "Isn't that what she told you?"

"Well, not technically. She said she was sure he had a girlfriend and she wanted to meet with me." I thought for a moment and tried to recall the exact conversation. "Maybe I'm overthinking our brief conversation. But she never said why she wanted to hire us."

Alex slid back into the passenger side. She turned to face me, with one leg tucked under the other on the seat. "What if there was something else? What if Jeffrey's affair was only a part of it?"

"I guess it's possible," I said. "But we'll never know."

Alex stepped out again and started toward her house. "Let me go change." She took a few steps then turned to the Jeep. "I don't have to get all dressed up, do I?"

I laughed and looked down at the clothes I had on. "Are you serious?" I turned off the engine and pulled the key from the ignition. "I have something in mind. In fact, you're fine the way you are. Maybe even a little overdressed."

"Let me just clean up. Give me five minutes." She headed for her house. "I'm going to let Raz out. Just keep an eye on him, okay?"

I grabbed two chairs from the Jeep and placed them down next to each other on the pier. I grabbed the cooler and put it down between the chairs. "Have you ever been here?" I said.

Alex looked around. "Not in a long time."

I nodded toward the red clouds in the sky. "You can't beat the sunset at Shands Pier." I pulled a couple of beers from the cooler, cracked the tops and handed one to Alex.

We both sat quiet for a few moments. Our chairs were so close to each other, our elbows just about touched. Neither one of us moved.

I had my eyes out toward the sky, the sun still up on the horizon but on its way down. "We haven't done this in a long time. Even when work is slow, everything we do together now is always about work."

She stared at me, but didn't respond.

I said. "It's like our relationship—our friendship—went backward."

She had a curious look on her face. "Backward?"

I sipped my beer. "Maybe that's the wrong word. We became friends through work, right? Then, I don't know. When we were both working for Bob Campbell we'd try to go out and have fun. It wasn't always about the job or the work we were doing."

"We never talked about work, because you hated working there."

I laughed. "Okay, that's a fair point."

We both sat quiet for a couple of moments.

I said, "It's just that, now, even when we're not at work, it's just about the only thing we talk about."

Alex looked at me, like she was trying to smile but couldn't.

I looked out toward the sun starting to set over the river and brushed my hand through the air. "You know what?" I shook my head. "Forget I said anything." I tipped my head back and emptied the can of beer down my throat. I could feel Alex watching me, but I didn't take my eyes from the horizon. I reached into the cooler and pulled out two more beers, cracked the tops and handed one to Alex.

She sat with one beer in each hand. Double-fisted. "It really is a beautiful spot. It's peaceful here." She finished her first beer and put the can under her chair, then stood up and walked to the railing across from us. She leaned into the railing for a moment with her back to me, then turned. With one foot up on the bottom rail, she said, "So, tell me if I have this right." She looked down for a moment. "What you're saying is we've gotten so focused on our work...somehow neither of us ended up with much of a personal life?"

I shrugged and looked up at her. "We don't have to talk about this anymore."

She stepped from the railing and folded her arms in front of her. "No, I want to."

I stared up at her, and knew I'd opened a can of worms. But maybe that wasn't such a bad thing. I said, "We used to do things like this all the time. But when we decided to focus on the business, well... It's what makes us both good at what we do. We're both focused. And the last thing I want to do is screw up the one thing that's working in my life."

Alex kept her eyes on me and kept quiet for a moment. "You think something's missing?"

I finished another beer, wished I'd brought a bottle of Jack and cracked open another. I raised my can to her in a toast. "You know what? Forget I said anything." I turned my eyes toward the setting sun. "Let's just enjoy the view...which is why we're here."

Alex stepped closer and stood right over me. She stared right into my eyes, her arms still folded. "Why do you do that?"

I cleared my throat. "Why do I do *what*?"

"You know exactly *what*. You've got something you want to say, but then you shut down...lock it all back inside where you think you're safe."

I looked at the can in my hand, then raised my gaze. "Maybe I need a break after this investigation. A breather."

Alex's eyes widened. She put her hands on her hips. "A breather? A breather from *what*? From work? From me?"

I shook my head. "Jesus, no. Not from you. Maybe from the business. The work. I don't know. I can't put my finger on what it is, but something's—"

"Is it the blackouts?" Alex sat in the chair next to me.

"It's been a long time since I had one," I said, leaning over to knock my knuckles against the wood on the pier. "The truth is, I don't have much else in my life. And if you and I are business associates and nothing else, then..."

We both stared straight ahead, looking out at the orange glow mixed with the blue sky.

I got up and went to the railing, leaning forward with the can of beer between my hands. My back was to Alex, but I felt her behind me.

"I appreciate your honesty," she said. "But, to tell you the truth, that's one of the most self-centered things I've heard come out of your mouth."

I turned to her "What? Why? I thought..."

She said, "We've built this business together and turned it into something. You were a one-man band. But you're not anymore. You don't get to just decide if you want to walk away or…" She made quotes in the air with her fingers. "'Take a breather.'" She huffed out a laugh. "You made it this far. You made it to where you said you've always wanted to be. You're well respected. Our *business* is well respected. But now, what? Are you having a midlife crisis?"

"Why are you getting so mad?" I said.

She stared at me, a crooked smile on her face. "Oh, I'm not mad. But I did think, at first, you were going in a completely different direction." She reached down into the cooler and pulled out another beer. "And, second—I never told you this—but, I could've joined the sheriff's office. But I didn't, because I knew you wanted me to work with you. I knew we made a good team."

She turned from me and walked to the other side of the pier. "Alex?"

With her back to me, she said, "You can't just decide to walk away."

I shook my head. "That's not what I meant. You know me better than that, don't you?"

She took a moment, then laughed. "Honestly? I'd need a degree in Psychology to figure out what's in your head sometimes."

I smiled, then sat back down in my chair. I cracked open another beer and leaned forward with my elbows on my thighs. I looked toward the orange sky, the sun moving fast behind the horizon. "You want to go get something to eat?"

She shrugged and sat down next to me. "I could eat. Or we could stay here and finish those beers."

Chapter 11

I WALKED TOWARD THE hotel being built just off route 200, a few miles from the St. Johns Town Center. A group of seven men stood around a truck, wearing hardhats.

"Excuse me," I said. I approached the men. "I'm looking for Emma Buckman. Any idea where I can find her?"

The men all exchanged looks. The man who appeared to be in charge turned and took a step in my direction. "What's that?"

"Emma Buckman? Any chance she's around here somewhere?"

The man cleared his throat and spit on the ground a few feet from where I stood. "Is she the good-looking architect?"

I nodded. "All I know is that she's the architect."

"Well, we don't deal with them over here. Not unless we really have to." He looked at the others and they all laughed.

I put my hands on my hips, not in the mood for any games. "You know where I can find her? Or no?"

He sipped what I guessed was a coffee from a styrofoam cup and gave me a nod in the other direction. "You'll have to find Bruce Rose, he should know."

"Bruce *who*?"

"Rose. He's in charge, works for the General Contractor. He gets to deal with the architects." He huffed out a laugh. "Although I hear he doesn't mind working with this one so much."

Again, the other men laughed but I wasn't sure I followed.

The man shrugged. "I'm sure he's around somewhere, but I haven't seen him all day." He pointed toward the building. "Maybe around back."

I walked away without another word then turned the corner around the building. I walked along a tall chain-linked fence and saw three men in hardhats standing in a circle on the other side of the fence. They all turned and looked at me.

I stared through the fence. "I'm looking for Emma Buckman. Or maybe Bruce Rose?"

A man with white hair under his hardhat stepped toward me from the other side and hung his hands on the chain linked fence. He slipped his fingers through the holes. "She the hot little thing, walks around here like she owns the place?"

I was about to respond, but didn't. "You know where she is?"

He turned over his shoulder and pointed toward a gray trailer far behind the hotel, almost on the other side of the lot. "If she's not in there, I don't know where she is." He turned and walked back to his small crew but then yelled for me when I started for the trailer. "Hey," he said with a crooked smile on his face. "You might want to knock."

I walked across the mud-covered grounds and approached the trailer. I tried to look in through the windows, but the blinds on the inside were closed. I reached for the door and tried the knob, but it was locked.

There was nobody around outside and most of the parking lot was filled with empty pickup trucks or pallets stacked with building material.

A man drove a forklift toward me and I stepped down from the door. He gave me a nod with his chin then drove toward a pallet and lifted it with the long, steel forks. He pulled away and drove toward the hotel without a word.

I walked around the back of the trailer, saw another door and pushed it open. Inside were three desks and long rolls of paper piled next to what looked like blueprints spread open on one of the desks. There was a laptop with a cup of coffee with steam coming off the top on one of the other desks.

I heard a voice from behind a door. It was a woman.

I walked toward the door and pushed it open. "Hello?"

The first thing I saw—but wished I hadn't—was a man's hairy, naked ass stuck up in the air. Underneath him, on a couch against the back wall, was a young woman whose face I recognized right away.

Emma Buckman's eyes were right on mine. She screamed.

The man jumped up from the couch and fell down to the floor, his pants down at his ankles. He screamed, "Get the hell out of here!" He pulled his pants up, his back to me. "What the hell are you doing in here?"

Emma covered herself with a shirt pressed against her naked chest.

I ran for the door, the man still yelling, but I couldn't make out what he was saying. I smashed the door open and jumped out of the trailer, running as fast as I could until I got to the three men on the other side of the fence. I stopped. "Excuse me," I said, "Is Bruce Rose the big guy with the beard?"

All three nodded and I gave a thumbs up.

"Found him," I said. "But I forgot to knock."

I got to the Jeep and called Alex, telling her what I'd just witnessed. "I have a feeling Emma might be more willing to talk to us now."

She said, "And you're sure it was her?"

"I could give you a full physical description if you want one?"

"Please, no. I believe you," she said. "And, you're sure it wasn't Jeffrey?"

"Absolutely not. This guy was much bigger…"

Alex laughed.

"Get your mind out of the gutter," I said. "I mean his *build*. He was a big man. Built like a house. Or, a lumberjack. He's the General Contractor, the GC, on the hotel Jeffrey's firm designed. Emma, I guess, takes good care of her clients."

Alex laughed, "How'd you find out she was there?"

"I called her office."

"And you're still there now?"

"I just got in the Jeep. If the guy could've gotten his pants on a little faster, I'm not sure he would have let me out the door."

"Nobody asked who you were?"

"No." I looked into my rearview and turned the key in the ignition. "Oh shit," I said. "There's a pickup coming toward me. It's probably him."

I pulled out of the hotel parking lot and slammed my foot on the gas. The pickup truck was coming up behind me.

I made a quick u-turn and headed toward the truck, but in the opposite direction, passing right by the driver. I saw the thick beard and confirmed it was Bruce Rose.

He screamed something out his window as we drove past each other. Before he could turn around, I took off down a side street and was gone before he had a chance to follow.

Chapter 12

ALEX WAS AT THE bar, away from the crowd. Billy was on the other side at the far end helping his customers, but came back and stood in front of me. He looked over his shoulder toward the crowd, as if making sure nobody would listen. He said, "Jeffrey Jenner was in here looking for you."

"Are you sure it was him?"

Billy nodded. "Yeah, it was him. He wanted to know how to get up to your office. But I told him you weren't in. And that it was by appointment only."

"Did he stick around for a drink?"

Billy shook his head, walked away and grabbed a couple of pints, filling them from the tap. He turned and carried the beers to his customers down the other end.

Alex took her laptop from her bag and opened it up on the bar. She showed me a grid she had laid out in a document with all the people she'd connected to Sarah. "You think we should add your new friend from the construction site to the board?"

"Yes, of course. His name is Bruce Rose. All I know so far is he looks to be in charge of that hotel off of route 200. And with Jeffrey's firm involved..."

Alex reached for her glass. "Clearly, he and Jeffrey must have a tremendous relationship." She cracked a grin and took a drink, then pushed the glass aside and typed on the laptop. "Let's see what we can find about Bruce Rose." She typed, then stopped and stared at the screen.

"You see something?"

She turned the laptop so I could see it. "Yes. He's good looking."

Bruce Rose had a neck like the trunk of a tree with a beard only a man in construction could get away with. "Your subjective view of his looks isn't exactly what I'm most interested in," I said.

"He also looks quite young," she said. "More Emma's age. I thought he'd be older." She squinted and scanned the screen on her laptop. "I just imagine the man in charge of a big construction project like that'd be more like a middle-aged man with a big belly."

"Okay," I said. "Can't we dig into something beside his good looks?"

Alex looked up from the laptop. "He also ran the project for the new Hendrick Logistics building."

I almost fell off the stool.

Billy walked over and stood in front of us. "Are you two going to eat?" He looked from me to Alex. "Is everything all right?"

"The guy I just caught on top of Jeffrey Jenner's young girlfriend works for the company that built Hendrick Logistics. That's where Sarah Jenner worked."

Billy shrugged. "Is that supposed to mean something?"

I shrugged. "Maybe. Maybe not. But he might've known Sarah Jenner. And maybe her friend, Kelly Swift. And Mickey Hendrick."

"Look at this." Alex turned the laptop so Billy and I could both see the screen. "It's a photo of the Hendrick Logistics ribbon cutting ceremony." She pointed to the screen and turned to me. "Isn't that him?"

Billy leaned in close. "Who?"

"Bruce Rose. The cute one with the thick beard."

I leaned-in toward the picture. "Look, that's Sarah. Standing right next to him. I'd say they're pretty friendly with each other...the way they're leaning into each other."

Alex pulled the laptop back in front of her. "He's right. The way she's looking at him in the picture..." She again pointed to the screen. "Kelly Swift's there, standing in the back."

Billy pulled the towel off his shoulder and wiped his hands. "So, Sarah Jenner's husband and this construction guy are both sleeping with the same woman?"

Alex and I both looked at him and nodded at the same time.

"And what about the poor woman who was killed. How does she fit into all of this? You think she might've been with the construction guy?"

"His name's Bruce Rose," I said. "And we have no idea how Sarah fits into any of this, other than her husband's mistress seems to get around."

Billy scratched his head then walked away toward the other end of the bar.

Alex gave me a look. "Let's not jump to any conclusions about any of this." She tapped the key on her laptop. "I'll try *Mickey-Hendrick-Bruce-Rose*...see how those two are connected."

Billy had already walked back to us and leaned on the bar. "Did I hear you say Mickey Hendrick? I knew I recognized that name when you mentioned Hendrick Logistics."

I looked up from the screen. "You know him?"

Billy shrugged. "He used to come in here, back when it was the old place. So it's been a long time."

"Do you know anything about him?" Alex said.

"He was never alone." He rubbed his chin. "I could be wrong, but it was always a different woman." Billy looked out toward the dining area. "He'd always ask for a table in the back corner, which usually meant a couple wanted to hide, keep to themselves."

I turned to Alex. "Maybe he wasn't as faithful to his wife as he wanted us to believe."

Jake walked out of the kitchen and handed two plates to Billy.

"Hey Jake," I said. He walked over and shook my hand. "Have you talked to Wyatt's dad since the other day?"

Jake's face turned a slight shade of red. "Why?"

"Well, he came here looking for me. And I'm wondering how he knew where to look."

Jake looked down toward the floor. "I'm sorry, Henry." He nodded. "He actually called me, asked me to be honest with him. He asked how I knew you."

I said, "So he didn't believe you the first time?"

Jake shrugged. "I guess not. He called my cell yesterday. I didn't know what to say. I was going to lie, but—"

I turned to Alex. "Maybe he saw me follow him to Emma's apartment. But why would he have his tongue down her throat right on the sidewalk if he knew I was watching him?"

Jake said, "I just told him you were friends with Billy. He already knew I worked here. I'm really sorry. I didn't mean to say anything."

"Don't worry," I said. "It's not a big deal."

Jake turned and looked toward the kitchen. "I hope I didn't—"

"Let it go, Jake. Forget it," I said. "You didn't do anything wrong."

He nodded, then went back into the kitchen.

I said to Alex, "I think I'll go visit Jeffrey. If he's looking for me, I might as well make it easy on him and show up at his door."

Chapter 13

I RANG THE BELL at Jeffrey Jenner's house and waited outside on the steps. I tried to get a look inside through the glass on either side of the door, but there didn't appear to be anyone inside. I rang it again, then turned when a white convertible Mercedes pulled in the driveway. Jeffrey was in the passenger seat and appeared to be laughing, at least until he realized it was me.

His eyes jumped to the young and beautiful Emma Buckman behind the wheel. She wore big, round sunglasses with a silk scarf over her head.

They both looked toward me through the windshield and neither said a word.

I had no doubt she knew exactly who I was, thanks to our brief meeting in the trailer at the construction site.

I walked toward them. I could hear Jeffrey tell her to go around me and pull in through the garage. She reached up toward her visor and the garage door behind me started to open.

But she still hadn't moved the car.

"What are you doing?" Jeffrey said. "Go around him."

I stepped in front of the car to prevent Emma from driving forward, unless she wanted to run me over.

I had a feeling she did.

I looked through the windshield at Jeffrey. "I heard you were looking for me?"

He stared at me for a moment, then slowly shook his head. "Why would I be looking for *you*?"

I turned my gaze to Emma. She had both hands on the wheel with the engine still running. When she glanced over her shoulder toward the rear of the vehicle, I had a feeling she was ready to spin the car around and get out of there.

But I walked to her door on the driver's side and extended my hand. "Have we met?"

She looked up at me, swallowed hard, and shook her head. "I... I don't believe so." I could see the redness take over her face.

"Henry Walsh." I said. "You really look very familiar. Are you sure?"

Her mouth opened slightly as if to say something, but nothing came out.

I pulled at my chin, as if in deep thought. I shifted my gaze to Jeffrey. "I hope you at least change the sheets before you take her up there." I said to Emma, "Doesn't it make you uncomfortable, knowing you're in the same bed his deceased wife slept in just a couple of days ago? I'd sleep on the couch, if I were you. I'm sure you've slept on a couch before, haven't you?"

Emma revved the engine, then whipped the Mercedes around the Jeep and pulled into the garage. She and Jeffrey stepped out of the car.

I stood just outside the door. "Jeffrey, I was hoping to talk to you. But maybe I'll come back another time." I turned and started to walk away, then looked back at him. "Hey, I didn't know your firm was involved in Mickey Hendrick's new building?"

Jeffrey turned and glanced at Emma on the other side of the car. "Hendrick Logistics?" He nodded. "Why? What does that have to do with?"

I said to Emma, "Did you work on that one too?"

She glanced at Jeffrey, but didn't answer.

"Is there a problem?" Jeffrey said. "We've worked on a lot of the construction projects in this town."

I crossed my arms. "Do you always work with the same general contractor?"

Jeffrey paused. "No. Not always."

"What about Sarah's role? Did she have anything to do with that project?"

Jeffrey paused again, taking his time before he replied. "I don't understand what you're getting at."

I thought it was a good time for me to get out of there, leave them both with something to think about. I stepped back from the entrance to the garage and headed for the Jeep.

They both stepped into the driveway and watched me climb inside and start the engine. I said, "Good seeing you again, Emma."

· · · · ● · ● · · · ·

Melinda was waiting for me at my boat when I pulled into my parking space. She was dressed differently than she'd been the last few times I saw her. She looked a little more relaxed with a tank top and shorts that showed off her fit legs.

"Thanks for coming by," I said. I walked past her. "I hope I didn't keep you waiting too long." I reached up over my boat and pulled down two folding lawn chairs, placed them both down on the dock.

"I haven't seen chairs like that in a long time," she said, running her hand over the green webbing on the aluminum frames. "Reminds me of summers, when I was a kid."

I laughed. "They belonged to my parents, but I took them from their house before they moved. Would've been cheaper to buy new ones after I had them re-strapped, but it wouldn't be the same. As long as the metal holds up…"

She sat down in the one I opened in front of her. I turned and stepped up onto the boat. "Would you like beer? A glass of wine?"

She shrugged. "Wine would be nice."

"Red or white?"

She turned and looked up at me, watching her from up on the boat. "White, if you have it."

I went down below, pulled a bottle of white wine from the small fridge in the galley. I reached for a couple of glasses and grabbed my bottle of Jack from the cabinet over the fridge.

I stood up on the deck and looked down at Melinda, her long legs crossed with both hands together on top of her thigh. She stared out toward the river. I wasn't sure if she knew I was there.

I stepped down and handed her the wine glass. I filled it for her from the bottle and said, "I don't drink wine, but I'm told this is good. A friend who used to own a boat I lived on at one time, before I got this one, sent me a case. It's from Australia."

Melinda took a sip and raised her glass.

I poured myself a double-shot of Jack and raised the glass to her then sat down next to her.

Melinda looked back and forth along the dock. "Is this what you do for fun? Sit out on the dock with your parents' old lawn furniture and drink whiskey?"

I shrugged with a smile. "Is there something wrong with that?"

She shook her head. "Please, no. Not at all. I envy your life, if this is how you live." She looked down into her glass, then lifted her eyes and met mine. "You seem like you kind of go by the beat of your own drum."

I looked over my glass at her and took a good sip of Jack.

"I've always followed the rules," she said. "I did the nine-to-five, did what I could to work my way to the top." She shrugged and let out a slight laugh. "Never got there."

I thought for a moment. "I work hard. But work is all I have. I don't think this is the life I had planned." I looked back at my boat. "But it works for now."

She sat still and watched me.

"I'll admit" I said, "sometimes I wonder if I missed something along the way. Maybe I was meant to get in line with everyone else, live the way we're told everyone's supposed to."

Melinda said, "You mean, follow along the way we're taught in school? To do what we're told and follow the rules for the rest of our lives?"

I nodded.

She sipped her wine and finished the glass faster than I'd expected. She at first seemed too uptight to be able to sit back and enjoy a drink. But I was wrong.

I reached for the bottle and filled her glass without asking, and she didn't seem to mind.

"See, I think maybe *I'm* the one who got it wrong," she said. "All those people out there, just like me." She looked toward the river. "I look around, and can't help but wonder if maybe you know something the rest of us don't."

I couldn't help but think about the conversation I had with Alex. And there I was, having what I thought was a similar conversation with Melinda. I don't think I started it, but I wondered what was going on in my head.

Maybe it was age.

I said, "I think as we start to get older, our thoughts start to change."

Melinda shrugged. "I used to overthink my future when I was younger. The future was all I thought about. Now, I feel like as we get a little older we spend more time looking back at the past. But some people, like you, seem to be able to live in the present better than the rest of us."

"Oh, I don't know if that's true," I said. "I don't mean to preach. But when you lose someone you love you can't help but think back on your life. The memories are all there, sometimes with more impact than our day-to-day lives."

Melinda stood from her chair and faced the river. "Sarah worked her whole life for her career. When she had Wyatt, she left to be a mom. But all she ever talked about was how much she missed work. She was afraid she'd never be able to go back."

"Did you know she was promoted to be a VP at Hendrick Logistics?"

She turned. "Her boss told me that."

"Mickey?"

"Yes. At Jeffrey's house."

"How come you didn't mention that?"

"I don't know. How did *you* know about it?"

"He told me, too. I understand he liked her very much." I turned to face her. "What about her friend, Kelly? Do you think it would've bothered her to see Sarah get such a big promotion?"

Melinda took a moment before she answered. "I don't know her well enough. But I do know she was responsible for getting Sarah hired. In fact, when Sarah first started, Kelly was pretty much her boss."

"So don't you think she could've been upset?" I said.

She stared me right in the eye. "Are you asking me if Kelly could have killed my sister because she was passed-over for a promotion?" She looked off, toward the river. "Don't take this the wrong way, but that's ridiculous."

Melinda sat down in the chair, reached for the bottle from the dock and poured herself more wine. She had her eyes down in her glass and ran her finger along the rim. "Sarah worked very hard. I believe she deserved that promotion." She looked up at me. "I don't know if Kelly ever worked half as hard as Sarah."

Chapter 14

For the first time in a handful of nights I was fast asleep in my bed when I woke up to footsteps out on my boat's dock. I leaned off the edge of my bed and grabbed a shirt, sat up and slipped it on over my head.

I reached for a signed baseball bat I received when I left my job with the Sharks and stood at the bottom of the ladder. I listened, then stepped with one foot onto the ladder. I looked up into the darkness above me and a shadow moved under the light along the dock.

I stepped back out of view and held the bat with both hands over my shoulders. I stood in the darkness down below and waited.

The light of a flashlight danced from above. A thick boot stepped onto the ladder's first rung.

As soon as the second foot stepped down, I flipped the lightswitch.

Bruce Rose jumped down off the ladder and lunged for me. I came up swinging the bat with both hands, but he ducked and reached for my throat with both hands. He tightened his grip and I choked, gasping for air.

I took another swing and cracked him in the leg with the bat. He reached for his leg with a scream, then came up and caught me with a left hook under my chin.

I fell into the counter behind me.

The burly man with his beard charged at me with his hands low, driving his shoulder into my chest. We both fell, and I drove one punch-after-another at his head.

But stopping him was like trying to stop a bull. He got up and lifted me by my feet, spun me on his shoulder and threw me onto the counter next to the sink. Dishes fell and smashed on the floor.

I locked my arm around his neck and twisted his head, prepared to rip it from his body if I had to. But my feet were still off the ground with my hand in the sink to keep me from falling back.

Bruce got a good hold of me and tossed me into the folding door to the head. The door snapped in half and ripped from the hinges. He reached out and grabbed me from behind, pulled with both hands and turned me around so he could punch me in the face.

It sent me stumbling backward and into the sink, where I reached for a bottle of Jack Daniels I'd left out on the counter. I had the bottle's neck in my grasp, and when he came at me again, I swung the bottle and smashed it over his head.

He looked at me with a blank stare, then stumbled back into the counter behind him. Bruce touched his head, looked at his bloody hand, then fell to the floor. He stayed in a seated position, his back up against the lower cabinet, legs straight out in front of him. Blood dripped down his face and into his beard.

I reached for a towel from the counter and tossed it on his lap. "You might want to get that looked at."

He reached for the counter and pulled himself up with both feet. With the towel against his head, I was sure he was done.

But I was wrong.

He came right at me with a wild swing and tried his best to throw a punch.

I ducked.

He missed and fell into the sink. As he turned around, I threw a punch and caught him in the back of the head. I hit him so hard I was sure I broke my hand on his thick skull.

But it must've hurt him as much as it hurt me, because he stumbled away, bloodied, and made it to the ladder. He climbed up and disappeared without looking back.

. . . .

Alex was at her desk early when I tried to sneak past her with my sunglasses down on my eyes.

She looked at me, her eyes widened as she rose from her chair. "What happened to your face?"

"Bruce Rose happened."

"The contractor?"

I pushed my sunglasses up onto my head, then reached inside my mouth to wiggle a tooth I was sure he'd knocked loose. "He showed up at my boat in the middle of the night." I walked to the kitchen area and poured myself a coffee. I took a sip and winced when the heat hit the cuts inside my mouth, taking the coffee to the couch.

I sat down and Alex came over, standing in front of me.

"What did he say?"

I shrugged. "I guess he didn't like that I caught him having sex with Emma."

She leaned over and pushed my hair away from my bloodied forehead. "Jesus," she said. "You're a mess." She straightened herself out and put her hands on her hips. "He didn't have a weapon?"

"Just his fists." I held up my hand and showed her my torn knuckles. "I got a few punches in, but it was like hitting a brick wall."

She walked into the kitchen area, pulled a towel from the drawer and ice from the freezer, walked back and sat down next to me, pressing the towel of ice against my head.

"You have a lump the size of a baseball," she said. "Actually, more than one."

"I wonder if Emma called him," I said. "After I saw her at Jeffrey's, I told him I gave her a hard time."

"So the guy just shows up, drags you out of bed and beats the crap out of you? Then he takes off?"

"He didn't drag me out of bed. And he didn't beat *anything* out of me. You should see what *his* face looks like."

Alex grabbed my hand and put it on top of the towel with ice against my head so I could hold it myself. She got up off the couch and walked back to her desk.

I said, "The thing is, as far as I can tell, this has nothing to do with Sarah. All I did was open a can of worms." I shook my head. "Like I have time to deal with this asshole." I stood up with the ice on my head and turned toward the window. I looked out at the St. Johns. "The guy had to've been angry enough to wake up in the middle of the night and show up at the marina, just to make a point?" I turned and looked back at Alex. "You think he has any idea she's also sleeping with Jeffrey."

Alex said, "I've been thinking about that."

"About what? Emma and Jeffrey?"

"Well, thinking about the fact it makes less and less sense that Sarah would need to hire us to prove he was cheating. It looks to me like everyone already knows."

"But maybe she just needed something more concrete," I said.

Alex stared back at me, her chin in her hand with her elbow down on her desk. "I think what you said yesterday, you might have been onto something. Maybe there was something else to it."

"You mean, she needed us for something else?"

We both stayed quiet for a couple of moments.

Alex said, "Don't you think we need to find out who else knew she called us?"

I nodded. "Besides Melinda, I don't know who else she would've told. She was supposed to meet Kelly, then come meet me after the gym. But it didn't seem like Kelly knew much about it."

Alex stared back at me. "Someone wanted to stop her from telling you. And killed her."

We both remained quiet in our thoughts until the phone rang a moment later.

I answered, "This is Henry."

"Henry? This is Jeffrey Jenner. I'm sorry about what happened earlier at my house. The fact is, you were right. It was me at your friend's bar. I was looking for you. I just didn't want Emma to know."

"Oh," I said. "Thanks for letting me know. I'm hanging up now."

"Wait!" he said. "Can you meet me? At Alexandria Oaks Park... FEC Park?"

"When?"

"Now?"

I looked at my watch. "You'll have to give us some time. My partner and I are just finishing up some—"

"I prefer you come alone," he said.

Chapter 15

ALEXANDRIA OAKS PARK IN San Marco was busy with a lot of people and even more dogs.

Jeffrey sat on a bench with a cup of coffee in his hand. His head was down in his phone when I walked up behind him. The First thing I did was look around to make sure I wasn't falling into some kind of a setup. I didn't trust Jeffrey Jenner. I sat down on the bench next to him. "So what's this all about?"

He kept his eyes straight ahead. "Why were you at my office, asking about Emma?"

"Did she tell you that?"

He shook his head. "No, she didn't. In fact I asked her what you meant when you left my house." He turned to me. "You said something to her, that it was good to see her *again*. But, I don't know why you used the word 'again' when she told me she didn't know who you were."

Part of me wanted to laugh, but what did I expect her to say? That I walked in on her and Bruce?

He crossed his arms. "But the way she looked at you, I have to admit I can't help but wonder if there's something she's not telling me."

Jeffrey sipped his coffee and didn't say a thing for a couple of moments. Finally, he turned to me again. He said, "I love her, you know."

I leaned against the back of the bench and looked across the park as if I hadn't heard what he said. But I could feel him stare at me. I'm sure he hoped I'd have something to say.

When I turned to him, he was still staring.

"What happened to your face?" He pointed to his own face, as if he was looking in a mirror. "What's that? You look like you've been in a fight."

I wasn't about to answer him. I knew I didn't have to. But I leaned forward on the bench then looked back at him over my shoulder. "Can you get to the point of this meeting? And tell me why you were looking for me at Billy's Place?"

Jeffrey reached into his pocket and pulled out an envelope. He handed it to me. "I'd like to offer you something."

I looked at the envelope in his hands but didn't take it from him. "What's that?" I said.

He held it toward me. "Take this. It's money. A fair amount, too. I want you to take it and leave me alone." He looked down toward the ground. "I have nothing to hide. There are no more secrets. Emma and I can be happy together now. I'd like you to leave us alone." He lifted his head and turned to me. "I know Sarah must've hired you. But she's gone now. I don't know if maybe you feel some kind of obligation to her, to prove I was having an affair, but..." He looked off, somewhere else, his eyes squinted from the sun. "Just take this. For whatever work you've done. I think it would be good if we could all move on with our lives."

My eyes were on his outstretched hand and the envelope he'd stuck in front of me. I stared at him for a moment. "I don't know if you're playing games with me or if I look like some kind of fool..." I nodded once toward the envelope and got up from the bench. "But I don't take bribes."

I got up and started back to my Jeep.

Jeffrey stood up from the bench and followed after me. "You're making a mistake. I promise you, I'll—"

"I don't take too kindly to threats, either," I said, stopping and turning to him. "And, if you'd really like to know, I'm not sure why your wife hired me. I don't know if it was because you were cheating on her. It didn't seem to be much work to prove it. But whatever she wanted me to do for her, I'm going to find out. And it might just turn out I'm the one who has to prove her death wasn't just an accident."

Jeffrey followed behind me. "What? Walsh. Wait a minute. Stop. What do you mean, *prove* it wasn't an accident?" He picked up his pace to catch up to me.

I said, "You're trying to bribe me to leave you alone. The only thing that tells me is you have something to hide."

He grabbed me by the arm. "If you're trying to tell me she was murdered, then—"

I yanked my arm from his grasp. "Then *what*? You'll do whatever it takes to shut me up?"

"No!" he said. "That's not it, I swear, I..."

I walked ahead, then turned to him, pointing to my nose. "See this thing? It's been bitten one too many times, because I've put it in places where it might not belong. But that's just what I do." I stood face-to-face with him. "I don't know if you had anything to do with what happened to Sarah, or what it is you're trying to hide." I looked down at the envelope, still in his hand. "Keep in mind, if you think I'm the type who'll stop doing my job so I can have a few extra bills in my pocket."

I stopped and walked away, got to my Jeep and hopped up into the driver's seat. I took off without saying another word to Jeffrey Jenner.

• • • • • • • • • •

I had already called Alex on the ride back to the office and told her Jeffrey had offered me a bribe to go away.

She looked up from her desk when I walked in. "Sounds guilty, doesn't he?"

I shrugged, grabbed a bottle of Jack Daniels from my desk drawer and sat down with a glass. "I don't know what I'm supposed to think. It would be too easy to say Jeffrey wanted his wife dead." I got up and grabbed two ice cubes from the freezer, dropped them in my glass and filled it with whiskey. "If you could've seen Jeffrey's face when I told him I thought Sarah's accident may not have been an accident."

I sat at my desk and Alex came over to me, placed a sheet of paper in front of me.

"What's this?"

"It's an old press release I printed, from Hendrick Logistics."

I quickly ran my eyes over the text.

Alex said, "Kelly Swift's husband was a business partner with Mickey Hendrick. Before he started Hendrick Logistics. Went bankrupt, and it looks like a lot of people lost a lot of money."

"Kelly Swift's husband?" I looked up at her. "Who is he?

"Ryan Swift. The one out in San Francisco."

"What's the significance?"

"Well, Hendrick took what was left of that business and turned it into Hendrick Logistics. And Kelly, for whatever reason, ended up working with Mickey Hendrick."

I stared at Alex, somewhat confused. "I guess I'm still not following..."

"Well, I don't know what happened with her husband or how that business fell apart. But Kelly was the first person Mickey had working for his company. Kelly, as she told us, was the one who hired Sarah. That was four years after Hendrick Logistics was started." Alex stepped toward me and sat on my desk. "Then Sarah gets a promotion that would've made her a VP, which essentially would've made her Kelly's boss."

I shrugged. "Doesn't that happen all the time in corporate America? People get passed over for promotions all the time."

Alex looked somewhat frustrated that I wasn't following her logic. "Don't you think it would cause some friction between Kelly and Sarah? And yet, according to Kelly, she and Sarah were still best friends..." She shook her head. "I don't buy it."

I said, "But we have no idea if Kelly even wanted that position. Maybe she's happy doing whatever it is she does?" I thought for a moment."Although, I didn't get the feeling she was the type to turn down a promotion."

Alex stepped down from my desk and walked across the office. She had her back to me and looked out the window toward the river.

I said, "Do you really believe this gives Kelly Swift a real motive? Because she got passed up for a job?"

She turned from the window. "Don't forget, she was the only person who was supposed to see Sarah that morning."

Chapter 16

ALEX AND I SHOWED up at Kelly Swift's front door around seven in the evening and hoped she'd be open to answering a few more questions.

I rang the doorbell. She opened the door like she'd already known we were there. With a glass of wine in her hand, she greeted us both and smiled before welcoming us inside.

We followed her down a hall toward the back of the house and into a living room area just off the kitchen.

There was some sort of reality show on the TV, a naked man and woman with their private parts blurred out on what looked to be a tropical island.

Kelly reached for the remote, pointed it toward the TV and turned it off. She said, "I don't normally watch shows like that."

"I hope you don't mind that we stopped by unannounced," I said. "But we'd like to continue our conversation from the other day, if that's all right?"

She drank what was left in her glass and placed it down on the counter. "I didn't realize we hadn't finished. Then I guess I can assume it's about Sarah?" She threw up her hands and turned toward her kitchen. "Oh, how rude of me. I'm sorry." She pointed her finger and wiggled it back and forth between me to Alex. "I hope this time you'll at least join me for a drink?"

Alex shook her head, and I had no choice but to do the same.

Kelly walked around the other side of the counter and into the kitchen, pulled a bottle of wine from the fridge and filled her empty glass. She placed the bottle down on the counter. "If you'd like a glass, just let me know." She gave me a wink and a crooked smile. "I have beer and liquor, too."

I decided to get right into it. "So, I understand you were one of the first employees Mickey hired to work for Hendrick Logistics?"

She nodded. "Not *one* of the first employees. I was *the* first employee."

I said, "And is it also true your husband started a business with Mickey Hendrick that went bankrupt? And what was left of it became Hendrick Logistics?"

Kelly stared back at me over her glass, taking a moment before she answered. "Well, that's not exactly how Hendrick

Logistics was started. It was a completely separate business from the one Ryan and Mickey had together."

I said, "So what happened to that business? The first one?" Kelly leaned with one hand down on the counter, the other with the glass in her hand in front of her. "Well, what happened was Ryan got caught with his hand in the cookie jar."

Alex glanced my way then said to Kelly, "Do you mean your ex-husband was stealing from the company?"

Kelly looked down into her glass. "Ryan stole from everyone."

"Is that why you got divorced?" I said.

She stared back at me and narrowed her eyes. "I don't know what my failed marriage has to do with any of this?" Kelly walked to the other side of the room and sat down on the couch. She turned and faced me and Alex then gestured toward a loveseat across from her. "Please, have a seat." She sipped her wine. "Are you sure I can't get you a drink?"

Alex sat down but I stayed where I was. I said, "Actually, I'd love a drink."

Kelly got up from the couch. She went to the counter and topped off her wine, then walked into the kitchen. She opened the doors to her pantry and flipped on the light inside. It was filled with enough liquor to stock a full bar. She turned and looked at me over her shoulder. "Whatever you'd like, I'm sure I have it."

I didn't hesitate a moment. "If you have any Jack…"

She smiled and pulled out a bottle. "Of course I have Jack Daniels." She flipped off the light and closed the door, pulled a glass down from a cabinet and again looked at me from over her shoulder. "How do you like it?"

"Two cubes of ice, please."

She turned and nodded with a smile. She nodded toward Alex, still seated but watching us from the loveseat. Kelly said, "Alex, you sure I can't get you something?"

Alex stood up and walked toward us. "I'm okay for now. But thank you." She caught my eye and gave me a look like there was something she didn't like. I didn't think it was that I was having a drink. But maybe it was.

Every once in a while, Alex would be in a mood that made me feel like I was working with my mother.

Kelly handed me the glass and brushed past me when she walked from the kitchen back to the couch. She looked back at me, then glanced down at the space next to her.

But I didn't bite. I sat down next to Alex and felt Kelly watching me.

Alex gave me another one of her looks and said, "Kelly, would you mind telling us more about what happened with your husband and the business he had with Mr. Hendrick?"

Kelly sipped her wine then rested the glass down on the coffee table. She slid one leg under the other on the couch.

"Well, I've known Mickey for a long time. I even knew him before I met my husband. And when things fell apart in the business, I was the one who knew who was right and who was wrong. So I had to make a decision. Not only personally, but for my career. So I stuck with Mickey. He almost lost everything he had, and it was all Ryan's fault. So I was there for Mickey. I helped him get his business off the ground."

"But you never had any kind of ownership stake?" I said.

She shook her head. "No, I just helped Mickey. It was his business. He was the owner. So many investors were burned from the failed business, he had to do everything with his own money...whatever he had left."

I sipped my Jack Daniels and leaned forward, placing my glass on the coffee table between us. "So if you were there from the very beginning, then didn't the fact you hired Sarah...yet she was about to be promoted to VP somewhat rub you the wrong way?"

Kelly was about to take a drink from her glass but stopped. The expression dropped from her face. She looked down into her glass and stayed quiet for a moment before she spoke. She shrugged, "I knew Sarah was a very smart woman from the day I met her."

"What does that mean," I said. "It didn't bother you?" I glanced at Alex then continued. "Wasn't Sarah going to be your boss with this promotion?"

Kelly took her time before she answered. She wouldn't look me in the eye. "I'll be honest with you. I learned the job on the fly. I didn't have the past experience like she did. She had the degree. She'd been a CFO at a very young age...before she had Wyatt." She picked up her glass. "Mickey liked her a lot. The past year or so he stopped giving me as much responsibility and handed it over to Sarah."

"That didn't bother you?" Alex said.

Kelly shook her head. "Sarah was my friend. Why wouldn't I be happy for her?" A tear came down her face. She got up and walked toward the french doors toward the back of the room and stood quiet for a moment. She had her back to us then turned. The tears were obvious. "If you are trying to say I killed my friend because I was jealous of a promotion she got over me..." She looked down at the floor and shook her head. When she looked up, she pointed her arm straight toward the front of the house. "I'd like you to leave." Tears continued down her face.

Alex and I both stood and walked toward her.

I said, "Kelly, you have to understand we're just trying to get our arms wrapped around all of this. We're not trying to point a finger. But we believe something happened to Sarah that wasn't an accident. And it's up to us to get to the bottom of it.

She wiped her tears with her hand then looked back and forth from me to Alex. "How can you be so sure it wasn't an accident?"

· · · · • · • · • · · ·

I could feel Alex watching me from the passenger seat, although my eyes were focused on the rearview mirror and the headlights close behind us.

"What is it?" she said. "You've had your eyes in that rear view."

I glanced at Alex. "There's an SUV that's been behind us since we left Kelly's."

Alex knew better than to turn around, and instead slouched down in her seat. She tried to get a look out the side view mirror. "You sure they're following us? It's a busy road. And it's dark out."

I didn't answer.

We crossed the Main Street Bridge and turned north onto Ocean Street, downtown. I almost pulled into the Salvation Army parking lot, but continued driving straight.

Alex sat up in her seat. "What are you doing?" She pulled down her visor and used the mirror to look toward the road behind us.

"I'm going to make sure whoever's behind us follows us into the park." I turned onto Orange Street then left onto Hubbard and pulled into Confederate Park.

What looked like a green SUV was still behind us.

I turned the Jeep around in the parking lot but the SUV stayed right behind us. I pulled back onto Hubbard.

"Can you see what kind of car it is?" Alex said.

"It's green. I think it's a Dodge Durango." As soon as I was back on the street I slammed my foot on the gas. The Jeep's engine screamed, like it didn't want to work that hard.

But the green Durango behind us stayed right on our tail, no matter how fast I drove.

I headed toward Eastside, and yelled, "Hold on!"

I yanked the steering wheel to the right and turned down route one.

Alex turned in her seat. "They're still on us!"

I looked in the rearview and saw the headlights coming toward us, like it was going to smash right into the Jeep's rear-end.

But at the last second it veered from the lane and into the breakdown lane.

I could see it now. A green Dodge Durango with windows tinted so dark it was impossible to see inside.

We were both driving at a good clip, just over eighty-miles-an-hour.

I didn't want to take my eyes off the road at that speed, but turned to my right. The Dodge's rear passenger window started to go down.

"What are they doing?" I yelled to Alex, the wind swirling inside the uncovered Jeep. I turned and took another quick glance and saw the barrel of a shotgun poke through the window's opening.

Before I had a chance to react, the shotgun fired.

Alex let out a scream and fell forward into the dash.

"*Alex!*" I yelled.

Blood came down her shirt. She held her shoulder and turned to look at me. She didn't say a word. She had fear in her eyes.

"Alex, hold on." I reached for her and pulled her back against her seat. "I'm going to slam on the brakes..."

She nodded and held onto the steel grab bar on the dash in front of her.

I slammed my foot down on the brake.

The green Dodge blew right past us. I struggled to maintain control of the Jeep and for a moment thought it would flip. The tires skidded and squealed. The steering wheel jumped in my grasp. I turned the corner almost on two wheels hard onto East Duval. With the pedal to the floor I jumped the curb and cut down North Liberty.

Blood came down Alex's arm. It was all over her hands.

Her eyes were closed.

I pulled into the Jacksonville Fire and Rescue station and laid on my horn. I screamed for help. "*Alex,*" I said in a more calming voice. I reached for her hand. "*Wake up! Alex, please...*"

She opened her eyes and looked toward five uniformed men and women running toward us from the fire station.

"*She's been shot!*" I yelled.

I stepped from the Jeep and got out of their way.

All I could do was watch them try to help her. Alex glanced at me with far away eyes, then closed them.

Chapter 17

I GOT UP FROM the chair in the waiting area at the hospital when Billy rushed toward me from the elevator. "How is she?"

"She should be okay. Shot her in the arm, just under her shoulder." I nodded toward the hallway. "Officers are in there now, talking to her."

I looked past Billy. Detective Mike Stone, a friend of Alex's with the Jacksonville Sheriff's Office, walked toward us.

"What the hell happened?" Mike said.

"Someone followed us through downtown, fired a shot from the back window. Got her right in the shoulder."

With his hands on his belt he turned and looked toward the officers outside Alex's room. "Well, she's as tough as they come." With a nod he cracked a smile, his lips tight together. "I don't need to tell you that."

"I'm just glad she's okay," I said. "I feel like I could have done something."

"Don't start blaming yourself," Billy said. "Doesn't do anyone any good at this point. And if you think we're about to give you any pity..."

Mike turned again, looked toward the officers down the hall. "Have you talked to any of them yet?"

I shook my head. "I was told you wanted to talk to me first."

Mike nodded. "So what'd you see?"

I told him what happened, about the Dodge Durango that'd followed us for a while until the back window went down and someone fired a single shot.

"You couldn't see anyone?"

I shook my head. "Saw the eyes through the back window, right before the barrel came out. But with the windows tinted so dark..." I looked at Mike. "I wish I could've followed them, but Alex was in no condition."

He shook his head. "Smart move, bringing her to the fire station." He looked down toward my waist. "You still don't carry?"

I shook my head. "Alex usually does. But not today, for whatever reason."

The officers walked from Alex's room and started in the other direction.

Mike said, "I'll catch up with you later," then hurried after them.

Billy and I went in to see Alex.

She was sitting up in the bed when we walked into the room. She gave us a smile I could tell was forced, and I wanted to give her a kiss on the forehead. But instead I just put my hand on her good arm. "I'm so sorry, Alex."

"Sorry?"

"I left you exposed, right there next to them. I should have—"

"Shut your mouth, Henry. Okay? You didn't do anything wrong at all. I got shot. And I'm happy to be alive."

Her bad arm was fully bandaged from below her elbow up around her shoulder.

She said, "Doctor said if the angle of the bullet had been off by ten degrees, somebody'd be making my funeral arrangements."

Billy looked surprised, "The doctor said that to you?"

Alex let out a slight laugh. "Not in those exact words, but I got the gist of what he was saying." She looked toward the window across the room from her bed. "I just wish I got a better look. It all happened so fast." She paused. "Although I can still see those eyes coming over the window before he fired. It was like they glowed."

"What about the bullet?" Billy said.

Alex looked at Billy. "You mean did they get it out?" She shook her head. "In-and-out." She turned her eyes to mine.

"They want to look through your Jeep. In fact I thought they were going to talk to you after they walked out of here, but..."

"Mike was outside," I said. "He left with the other officers, although..." I looked toward the door then reached out and pushed it closed. "Did you tell them anything else?"

"No. I told them we're working on some different cases, and you never know who wants to get us out of their way."

"They didn't ask about anything specific?"

"No."

I sat on the edge of Alex's bed. "You find it more than a coincidence we'd just left Kelly's house?"

Billy said, "Who's Kelly?"

I said, "She's a friend of Sarah's, the one who was supposed to meet her to work out the morning of the alleged accident. And, now we're starting to wonder if there was something more to their relationship than just a couple of friends from the office."

There was a knock at the door.

Mike walked in and looked down at Alex. Billy and I stepped out of his way and he put his hand on her good shoulder. "We'll find them," he said. He turned to me. "No plate, is that right?"

I took a moment then nodded. "I tried. If I could've gotten behind them, believe me..."

Alex winced when she tried to sit up a little straighter in the bed. "They knew who we were. And they knew what they were doing."

Mike pulled a chair over from against the wall and sat down on the side of the bed. He looked at me, then over to Alex. "Either of you want to tell me what you were doing? I heard you're involved in a few different cases right now, but..."

I gave him a quick shrug. "We were just out, not really doing anything specific at the time."

He looked at Alex. "Okay, maybe you can give me an answer that has a little less bullshit." He raised both his eyebrows, waiting for her to answer.

Alex glanced at me..

Billy said, "They were supposed to meet me for a drink, down at Haden's."

Mike looked at Billy and kept his gaze on him for a moment. He squinted, a look I was sure Mike practiced at home, watching the old detective shows. "Haden's, huh?"

Alex said, "That's all it was. I guess you never know. A lot of crazies out there today."

I wasn't sure Mike was buying any of it.

He crossed his arms, looking at each of us, one at a time, as if someone was going to tell him the truth. We all just stared back until he walked for the door and pulled it open. But he didn't leave. He nodded toward me and Billy. "Would you both mind giving me and Alex a few minutes alone?"

"Uh... Sure," I said.

Billy and I left and walked down the hall. I glanced into each room we walked past and said to Billy, "I always think about each person's story in a hospital. You never know what lands you in here. Or who came in feeling a little sick, hoping to get some pills to clear it out. Doctor says you have three months to live, and you're not going home."

Billy had a perplexed look on his face. "That's what you think about?"

I didn't respond.

"Hey," I said, "I appreciate you helping us back there. For a moment I thought maybe we really did forget to meet you for a drink. Had me fooled too."

Billy said, "Yeah, but I'm not sure the detective actually bought it."

I nodded. "Probably not." We continued past the nurse's station and I said, "I don't know what it is, but usually I'm a lot better on my feet than I've been lately. Sometimes I wonder if my brain's working the way it used to."

"You're just getting older," he said. Then stopped. "Is it because of your mother?"

"I don't know.. Maybe. It *is* hereditary, you know."

Billy shook his head. "They don't know that for sure. They don't know half of what they'd like to know about diseases. That's the truth. We're a long way off from having all the answers."

We walked in silence then stepped onto the elevator. The doors closed and I pushed the button for the lobby.

Billy said, "So why don't you want Mike to know you're investigating Sarah Jenner's accident?"

"Well, I guess I've learned over the years to be more careful. It's not worth the friction it causes. Mike cares a lot about Alex, but the last thing he wants is for me to get in the way of the work the sheriff's office is doing."

"Even if they got it wrong?"

· · · · ● · ● · · · ·

Three officers were standing outside on the sidewalk next to the revolving door at the front of the hospital.

One of the three who had a good four inches on me looked like he was fresh out of high school. We started past them and one said, "Mr. Walsh? Mind if I take a look at your Jeep while you're here? Might need to have you bring it down to the station, but Detective Stone thought you'd be okay if we took a look right now." He looked around, then leaned his head down toward me. "You know, cut out some of the red tape."

I nodded. "Yeah, of course." I stepped along the sidewalk and pointed toward the side parking lot. "It's right over there. Parked up on the grass. But I'm kind of in a hurry."

Billy said, "I'm heading back to the restaurant. I'll see you back here in a little while." He took off in the opposite direction.

I walked with the young officer toward my Jeep. "I assume you're looking for a bullet?"

With a nod, he said, "Yes sir."

I gave him a look but didn't say anything about that. Even though the young officer was simply showing respect, being addressed as a *sir* made me feel old.

I pointed toward the Jeep. "There it is."

He stepped toward the passenger side, the seats still covered in blood. He leaned in and within a few seconds he'd spotted the hole in the passenger seat. He stepped back and looked at the back of the seat from behind. "They were ahead of you?"

I nodded. "Barely."

"She got shot through the front, right?" He pointed to the front of his own shoulder, just above his chest.

"I believe so. Yes."

He stepped toward the back seat again, looked up and down along the backrest. "The bullet didn't come out."

He stepped to the front again, nodded toward the seat then turned to me. "Someone dug that bullet out of the seat."

Chapter 18

I WAITED IN THE parking lot outside Hendrick Logistics, hoping Mickey Hendrick would pass by on his way into the office. I had already tried the doors, but they were locked.

I was told Mickey was the first one in every day, by six thirty.

It was six twenty-six.

A silver BMW pulled into the empty lot and parked in the spot closest to the door. Mickey Hendrick stepped out with his head down and a briefcase in his hand. He gave me a nod then walked past me toward the front door of his building. He stuck his key in the lock and pulled open the door.

He turned the lock from the inside and I knocked on the glass.

He squinted his eyes and watched me, staring for a moment before he pushed it open. "You're that private investigator, aren't you?"

I nodded and slipped in through the door. "Yes, sir. Henry Walsh."

"I'm sorry I ignored you out there. Homeless come around once in a while, looking for money."

I hadn't shaved in days. And the clothes I wore weren't exactly what you'd see around most corporate office parks. I said, "Do I look that bad?"

He laughed. "No, that's not what I meant. But, do you mind telling me what you're doing here this early in the morning?" He looked out through the glass door. "And where's your better half? What was her name? Alex?"

"Funny you should ask," I said. "She's in the hospital with a bullet wound."

Mickey's eyes opened wide. "She was shot? Are you kidding?"

"I wish I was. But I can tell you this: somebody doesn't want us asking anymore questions about what happened to Sarah."

Mickey's gaze moved toward the elevator. "Well, if it wasn't an accident, I hope you find whatever you're looking for." He reached out to shake my hand. "I'm sorry to cut you short, but I have to get up to my office. I hope you don't mind."

I ignored his gesture. "Actually, I do mind. I came all the way here, bright and early so we could talk. I need to ask you about Kelly Swift. I mean, not just Kelly. Her husband too. What I'm really wondering is how Kelly helped you get this business off the ground, yet Sarah was going to be promoted, to become Kelly's boss?"

Mickey stared back at me for a moment before answering. "I don't know what you want to hear. You seem to know enough already."

"Enough?" I shook my head. "Not quite. So why don't you go ahead and tell me?"

He shrugged. "I don't know what you expect me to tell you. There's not much to say about her husband, other than he single handedly destroyed my first business. Our business, at the time. And he left Kelly high-and-dry when he took off for the West Coast. She needed a job, and had a decent background in bookkeeping."

"So how does someone who'd been with you from the start lose out on a promotion like the one you gave Sarah?"

Mickey turned and looked toward the elevator. "Are you asking me an actual question? It sounds to me you seem to think you already have something figured out. And if you think any of this has something to do with Sarah's accident—which I assume is why you're even here—then you're sadly mistaken." He nodded toward the exterior glass doors. "You can show yourself out, Mr. Walsh. Before I have to have someone escort you out."

I put my hands up in front of my shoulders, my palms out toward Mickey. "I don't see the need for your hostility. Unless, of course, you have something to hide?"

Mickey put his briefcase down on the reception desk and stepped toward me. He folded his arms at his chest. "I don't know who you think you are, but you're starting to come off like you're making some kind of a threat? Is that what you're doing?" He narrowed his eyes. "I know you don't know a lot about me, but I don't take kindly to people making threats, trying to intimidate me."

We both stared at each other. I wanted to roll my eyes or clap for his brave performance, but I didn't. Without saying another word, I turned and walked outside.

· · · · ● · ● · · ·

Alex was already dressed and waiting for me in a padded chair when I walked into her room at the hospital. "I'm just waiting for the nurse, then we can go."

I sat down on the edge of her bed. "How are you feeling?"

She turned and looked out the window. "I think I felt better yesterday. Mentally, I'm a little drained."

"Drained?" I gave her a smile and she turned from the window. "I'd say there's a little more to it." I got up and walked toward her. "I want you to take as much time as you need. I don't mean just physically, but, you know, I want you to feel right. No need to rush back."

She rolled her eyes. "I'll be fine."

"I know. But I also want you to take whatever time you need."

"So did you find anything yet?" she said, clearly trying to change the subject away from her.

"I went to see Mickey Hendrick this morning. Bright and early, before he even showed up for work. That southern charm he likes to put on seemed to disappear." I looked past her toward the window and the blue sky outside. "I asked him about the promotion, and why he'd promote Sarah over a woman who'd worked for him since day one."

Alex came and sat next to me on the bed. "Did he give you a good reason?"

I shook my head. "He didn't say much at all." I turned and looked at Alex's shoulder, still bandaged down to her elbow. "So what did you tell Mike?" I said. "You tell him what we're working on?"

Alex shook her head. "No, but I hate lying to him. Although the truth is, the last thing we need is pushback from Mike. He'd make it very difficult on us."

We both looked up at the TV hanging from the wall.

I said, "Did Mike mention anything about the bullet?"

"You mean that they couldn't find it?"

"Yes, but also that the officer I was with said it looked like the hole had been picked-at. Someone came right here to the hospital while I was in here with you, dug through the seat and took the bullet. So I went by the station, and sure enough the officer was right. Someone cut it out of the seat."

Alex got up off the bed and winced in pain. She grabbed her injured shoulder.

"They give you anything for the pain?" I said.

She shook her head. "Nothing I'm going to take."

Chapter 19

Emma Buckman arrived home late in the evening. She pulled into the parking lot outside her condo and I sat in the Jeep watching her. I was hesitant to approach too fast. After all, it was dark. And I didn't need to startle her.

You never know.

She stepped from her car and looked around when I called her name. First thing she did was reach into her purse. She pulled out a small spray bottle and held it up in front of her then turned in my direction, pointing it my way.

I was sure it was pepper spray and raised my hands. "Wait! Don't! It's me. Henry Walsh. Please don't spray that."

She kept the bottle up toward me, her eyes squinted. "Oh, you mean the stalker. If anyone should get this in the face, it's you."

I took a small step closer. "Can we talk?"

After she paused for a couple of moments, she put the spray back in her purse. I moved closer but she didn't take her eyes off of me.

"Are you alone?" I said.

She hadn't yet pulled her hand from inside her purse. "That's kind of a creepy question to ask a woman in a dark parking lot."

I looked up toward the lights overhead. "They really should make them a little brighter." I eased my hands down by my side. "I'm just here to talk."

She pointed her remote toward her car. The look on her face eased and the trunk lid popped open. She stepped to the back of her car and reached inside, pulled out a duffle bag and hung it over her shoulder.

"Can I help you with that?" I said.

She gave me somewhat of a crooked smile. "Are you looking for an excuse to come into my home?"

I shook my head. "I'm just offering to carry your bag."

"I don't know what else you need to know. I think you already know more about me than I'd like you to."

"I'm not here to get involved in your love triangle. I'm here because my partner was shot. She's lucky to be alive."

"I'm sorry to hear that." Emma turned and started toward the entrance to her building. "But what does that have to do with me?"

I didn't answer, because I wasn't sure. "Your friend Bruce Rose showed up at my boat in the middle of the night. And it wasn't to see if I'd take him out on the river."

"Is that what happened to your face?"

I touched one of the handful of bruises. "Are you going to tell me you know nothing about it?"

She pulled the door to her building open and turned, gave me a look over her shoulder and shook her head without giving me much of an answer.

· · · · ● · ● · · · ·

It was small but spacious inside Emma's condo. Everything was out in the open but a bed. There were no dividing walls other than the exposed brick on the perimeter of the place. The ceilings were high with canned lights hung from a metal rack, pointed toward the floor.

I turned and looked toward the window overlooking the bright, blue lights of downtown's skyline.

Emma pulled the cork from a bottle of red wine. "Would you like a drink?"

I shook my head. Red wine was never my drink of choice. "Thank you. But I think I'll hold off for now."

She was, without a doubt, an attractive woman. She was tall and beautiful and in exceptional shape. At least from what I could tell. But the problem I had—aside from the fact she was nearly half my age—is that she *knew* she was attractive. From what it seemed, Emma was the type to use her good looks to get whatever she wanted. And men like Jeffrey Jenner and Bruce Rose obliged.

Emma sipped her wine and leaned with one hand on the kitchen island between us. "I know what you must think of me," she said.

"Do you care what I think?"

She gave me a look and tipped her head back to finish her whole glass of wine. She held up the bottle before she re-filled her glass. "You sure you don't want any?"

I shook my head. "I'll be honest. I'm a little curious about your career track. I don't mean to take away from your skills or your knowledge. But for someone who's almost fresh out of college, I have to wonder why you're sleeping with two men who clearly have helped grease your track." I put up my hands, my palms toward Emma. "I mean your *career* track."

She stepped away from the island and leaned back against the counter behind her. She crossed one leg over the other, her arm crossed in front of her with her glass in one hand. "Jeffrey was my mentor. It's not unheard of for a woman to fall for an older man she respects and looks up to in a professional manner."

"Are you in love with him?"

She sipped her wine and her eyes moved toward the floor. It took her a couple of moments to answer. "Why should I answer that?"

"Well, if you love him. Then I guess I'd have to say perhaps you'd be one of a few people who wouldn't mind seeing Sarah Jenner dead."

Her eyes shot back at mine. She placed her wine glass on the island and leaned forward, both hands down in front of her. "You think I killed his wife?"

"Well, I asked you a simple question. If you can't answer it, then I have to assume maybe you have something to hide."

She shook her head. "I did not kill Sarah."

"Okay. Then let me ask you again. Are you in love with Jeffrey Jenner?"

She picked up her glass and sipped her wine. She turned and looked off toward the large square window. "I thought I was at first."

"But you're not now?"

She turned back to me and closed her eyes. She gently shook her head. "He needs me now."

I huffed a slight laugh out my nose. "How sweet." I folded my arms at my chest and rolled my eyes. "Okay, so if you're telling me you're not in love with him...and you're saying he needs you. Does that mean he's in love with you? Has he ever told you that?"

She stared back at me but didn't respond.

She picked up her glass and held it up in front of her mouth. "Jeffrey didn't kill Sarah, either."

I waited a moment, watching her sip her wine. "Either?"

"Well, I assume you believe I'm a suspect because I was sleeping with her husband." She shook her head. "I'm not a murderer, Mr. Walsh."

"Where were you the morning of her alleged accident?"

She looked down into her glass. "I was here. With Jeffrey." Her eyes moved toward a door I assumed was her bedroom. "He'd come over here every day. He'd tell Sarah he was going into work."

"What time?"

"He'd usually be here by six, a little before, then leave and get into work ahead of me, by seven, seven-thirty."

"Was he here when he got the call?"

"About the accident?" She nodded. "I was getting in the shower."

"So he told you?"

"He did, but he didn't know at the time she'd been killed. He left right away."

"When did you find out she was dead?"

She stared back at me for a moment before she answered, then shrugged a shoulder. "He called me. I don't know. Maybe around eight in the morning."

"The accident occurred well before six. Between five and five-thirty in the morning."

Emma stared back at me, but didn't say a word. She held her long fingers on the stem of her wine glass resting on the island's marble top.

"What was he like when he came over? I mean, how did he act?"

She narrowed her eyes and stared across the island. "If you think I'm going to help you try and pin such a tragic accident on Jeffrey, then I'm sorry." She shook her head. "I'm not going to help you." She threw back what was left of her wine and filled it again from the bottle.

"I don't know if he did it or not. But if you're not willing to answer some simple questions, then I'm sorry. We're right back to where we began, where I have to wonder what it is you're trying to hide."

She paused, then looked away with a slight sigh. "No, he didn't act differently. He was happy to see me, like he always is." She seemed to not want to look me in the eye

"Is there something you're not telling me?" I said.

She waited, then shook her head. "No."

Chapter 20

Alex was on her couch, her legs up on the coffee table when I let myself into her house. She had her laptop in front of her. Her dog Raz greeted me with his nose jammed into my crotch.

I handed Alex a cup of tea I'd picked up for her on the ride over. "I called you last night after I left Emma Buckman's apartment."

She opened the top of the tea. "I was going to wait up, but I was too tired. I actually turned my phone off. I slept a few hours, but I think I kept waking up."

"But you got my message?"

She nodded and blew into her tea. "I've been looking all morning. Since I got up."

I looked down at her shoulder. "How's it feel?"

"Not great. I think that's what kept me up, every time I rolled over. And I kept seeing those creepy eyes."

I sat down on the couch next to her. "At least it's something though, right?"

She turned to me. "What is?"

"The eyes. I only got a quick glance, but if you see them again you'll know it, right?"

"I just wish I'd had my gun. I would've at least got a shot off." She looked down at her laptop. "I did a little more research into Kelly and her husband. And Mickey Hendrick. Turns out, her husband was never arrested or punished for what they said he'd done. Nothing was ever proven, even though Mickey said Ryan Swift destroyed their company." She turned. "But it wasn't just Mickey Hendrick who lost a lot of money. They had private investors."

Raz sat on the floor and leaned against my leg. I said, "Was it investigated as a crime?"

Alex nodded. "Somewhat, yes. But, like I said, charges were never filed. And, of course, Kelly's husband Ryan Swift adamantly denied he had anything to do with destroying the company."

I got up off the couch and looked out the window toward the front of Alex's house. "I still don't get how Kelly ends up working with Mickey, after all that happened." I turned from the window. "So how do we find Ryan Swift?"

"Well," Alex said. "That's one of the problems. I haven't been able to locate him. I've never found someone without much of a digital footprint."

"Even in that dark web you use?"

She nodded. "I'm still working on it. But, like I said, it's rare I can't find at least something. Everybody with a pulse has some sort of trackable data...unless they've taken every step possible to make sure they can't be found."

I sat back down on the couch and leaned forward. Raz stuck his big head under my arm. "What if Sarah found something at Hendrick Logistics?"

"Like what?"

I thought for a moment. "I honestly have no idea."

Alex kept her eyes on me for a moment but didn't respond.

I said, "What if there's something she found that had something to do with Kelly's husband?"

Alex made a face and rolled her eyes. "Are you saying this because you're trying to come up with a motive for Kelly."

"Well, it did seem like that Durango showed up right after we left Kelly's house. Don't you think that's more than just a coincidence."

We both sat quiet for a moment.

Alex said, "But this whole thing started with Jeffrey Jenner cheating on Sarah. And then he tries to bribe you to go away."

"Emma Buckman was pretty convincing. I don't doubt she's a little manipulative, but she provides Jeffrey with an alibi. He was at her house at the time of Sarah's accident."

· · · · · • · • · · · ·

Melinda looked at me from across the table at Billy's Place. She sipped her wine then held the glass in front of her mouth. "It must take some discipline to have your office upstairs from a bar?"

"Sometimes," I said. I straightened out in my chair. "If you're not comfortable discussing things down here, we can—"

"This is fine." She looked down into her glass. "I know you said it could be a challenge trying to find the truth behind what happened to Sarah. But, why are you so hesitant to go after Jeffrey?"

I took a moment before I answered. "Because I can't just 'go after' someone. It's my job to find the truth. And right now, we have little proof. The fact he was cheating on Sarah isn't close to being enough." I sipped my drink and looked back at her over my glass. "When you first came to me, you were already convinced Jeffrey was behind it. But, you have to trust me that I'm turning over every stone. And, right now, there are other people we're focusing on."

Melinda stared back at me from across the table. She was quiet for a moment. "Don't let Jeffrey fool you."

"Don't worry. He's not fooling me."

"But you honestly believe he had nothing to do with it?"

I shook my head. "That's not what I said. But he's far from the only suspect. I wish I could reach into a black hat and pull out the name of the person who was responsible. But it doesn't work that way."

I could see in her eyes she didn't like what I'd said. And I started to wonder if there was more to it. If there was something she wasn't telling me. "Did Sarah talk to you about her job?"

She shrugged. "We talked about a lot of things."

I thought about it. "Well, here's what bothers me," I said. "Her friend Kelly hired her, right? And Kelly had been part of Mickey's company since the very beginning. Yet, Sarah gets a promotion that would've made her Kelly's boss? And when I asked Mickey about it, he was a bit defensive."

Melinda shrugged. "But people get leap-frogged all the time in corporate America. You know how many times I've been passed over for a promotion?"

I nodded. "But this is different. How much do you know about Kelly's husband? Did you know he was the one who started the original company with Mickey Hendrick, before it was Hendrick Logistics? Allegedly, Kelly's husband was blamed for the company's losses, which—as I understand—was quite a bit of money. Then Kelly's husband disappears...and Kelly ends up working with Mickey to get the new business off the ground."

Melinda stared back at me and slowly shook her head. "That's the first I'm hearing of it." She finished her drink and put her purse over her shoulder. She stood up from the table. "I'm sorry, I don't understand what any of this had to do with Sarah."

Chapter 21

I SAT OUT ON the dock and watched the dark sky over the St. Johns. I had nothing but my old folding lawn chair and a bottle of Jack to keep me company. Which was normally all I needed.

But it was hard to relax because, as much as I hated to admit it, I was lost. I was no further ahead than when I'd started investigating Sarah's death.

I had my suspects, of course. Although I knew I had to use the word *suspects* lightly. Because, all I really had were a handful of people I'd questioned. But none had a strong enough motive to be true suspects.

I pulled my phone from my pocket and dialed Alex. "Hey, how are you feeling?"

"Better."

"I was going to call you earlier, see if you wanted to come sit out by the dock. But I figured you needed another day."

"I've got cabin fever," she said. "So I might've taken you up on it."

I looked at my watch. "Is it too late?"

She laughed. "It's not too late. But I'm in bed. Me and Raz. I figured one more good night of sleep I should be ready to help a little more than I have."

I finished off what was left in my glass. "Would you mind helping me think through something? Or do you want to sleep?"

"Whatever you need," she said. "I'm awake."

"I was just thinking, we don't really know what things were like between Mickey and Sarah. What if, by chance, there was something between them? I mean, Mickey didn't like me questioning their relationship, and tried to make it clear he was faithful to his wife. But then Billy said Mickey used to go to his restaurant, and wasn't always with the same woman. So there goes his argument that he was faithful."

"You're making quite an assumption without any evidence," Alex said.

I held the phone between my shoulder and my ear then grabbed the bottle of Jack and filled my glass.

Alex said, "I was actually thinking about what you said earlier, about that Durango showing up after we left Kelly's."

"That's certainly suspicious. But I'm having a hard time believing she'd kill her friend because she was passed over for a promotion. And she didn't seem to be bothered by it."

Alex said, "You've been at this long enough to know people kill for a number of reasons."

Neither one of us spoke for a moment.

"I wish we had something more to bite into. I still don't believe Jeffrey has much of a motive. Men leave their wives all the time without having to drive them into a creek."

Alex didn't respond, and I wondered if she'd been listening to me. "Alex?"

"Sorry, yeah. I'm here. I think I just found something."

"Found something *where*?"

"Online. I think I just found Kelly Swift's husband."

• • • • • • • • • •

I walked into Alex's house and sat down next to her on the couch.

She turned her laptop toward me. "This is him."

"Ryan Swift?" There was a woman in the photo standing next to him. "Who's she?" I said.

"His wife. They own a bookstore together in San Francisco."

"Must be doing all right, if they can afford to live out there, running a bookstore. I thought they'd all gone out of business."

Alex said, "Who knows? Maybe he had money left over from whatever happened with Hendricks."

I said, "It sounds to me like he didn't walk away with any money at all. But I guess you never know."

Alex tapped on the keys on her laptop. "This is the website for the bookstore. Called Bayside Books. But he's not mentioned on it at all. I already told you, he's practically non-existent online."

Alex got up from the couch and walked in the kitchen. She came back with a beer and put it down in front of me. She already had a drink of her own on the coffee table in front of us.

I reached for the beer. "Maybe we should call?"

Alex looked at her watch. "West Coast time...they're open for another hour."

I grabbed my phone and dialed the number from the website. A woman answered right away and I asked for Ryan.

A moment later a man's voice came on the phone. "Hello?"

"Is this Ryan?"

"Who's this?"

"My name's Henry Walsh. I'm a private investigator. I'd like to ask you some questions."

There was quiet on the other end of the line.

"Questions about what?" he said.

"The business you had with Mickey Henrick."

The line went quiet again. "I have nothing to say." He paused. "You said you're a private investigator? Working for who?"

"Well," I said, "I'm not sure that's important. But I will tell you I'm investigating the death of a woman who worked for Mr. Hendrick."

"Oh," he said. "Did Mickey kill someone?"

"I'm not exactly sure that's the case," I said. "But, I would like to hear what you can tell me about Mickey and your ex-wife."

"Kelly? Does she have something to do with it?"

"I can't answer that. But the woman who was killed was a friend of hers."

"I'm surprised to hear that."

"That she was a friend of Kelly's?"

He let out a slight laugh. "I'm surprised Kelly has a friend."

I turned with the phone up to my ear and gave Alex a look. I said into the phone, "I take it you don't talk to her anymore?"

"Kelly? Why would I? I try not to even think about her. If I could forget her for the rest of my life, I would."

I heard someone else through the phone, talking to Ryan.

"Hold a moment, please." The sound through the phone was muffled, like he'd covered the mouthpiece with his hand. He came back on the line. "Sorry about that. All I was going to say was that Kell and Mickey and whatever you might've heard happened is in my past. I've put it all behind me as much as possible." After a brief pause, he said, "How'd you find me?"

"It wasn't easy. But I did. And now that I have, I'm just hoping you can shed a little light on what happened with you and Mickey. I realize charges were never filed but, according to your ex-wife, you were caught stealing from the business you had with Mickey."

"Well, that's what she likes to tell people. But it's not true. I never had anything to do with that money disappearing. That's why I was never charged. Even the cops knew I didn't do it. The fact is, I was on the technology side of the business. I was never even near the money. And I never had any direct connection with those investors."

"You mean, the investors who lost the money?"

After a brief pause, Richard said, "Yes."

"How much was lost?"

"Three million disappeared, like it never existed."

"And nobody was ever charged?"

"No. But as you've heard…they've blamed me. Ruined my career and my reputation."

"Who put the blame on you?" I said. "Mickey?"

"And Kelly. I swear. They set me up. And I had a lot of people coming after me. Even though there wasn't an ounce of evidence, Mickey made sure the investors all believed it was me, that I had their money somewhere."

"So you took off for the West Coast?"

"If I hadn't, I'd be dead. There were a lot of unhappy people. Mostly Mickey's friends who had invested with us. That's why he had no choice but to point the finger at me."

We were both quiet for a couple of moments.

"You really think Mickey and Kelly set you up? Does that mean you think the two of them might've been responsible?"

"You mean, did Mickey and Kelly take the money? I have a hard time believing they didn't take the money. But I had no proof, other than Kelly was the one running the books. And the two of them... I'd be shocked if they weren't sleeping together."

"Mickey and Kelly?" I said.

"I never caught them or anything. But it was almost too obvious at the time. Anything she wanted, she would get. The way he treated her..."

I got up from the couch and looked out the window into the front yard of Alex's house. I said to Ryan, "The woman who died... She worked for Mickey. She worked in finance with Kelly. And she'd recently been promoted to CFO. Meaning she'd be positioned over Kelly."

"Kelly's smart like that. When she was working with us, she and Mickey decided to keep her off the payroll. Looking back, I wonder if it was so she wouldn't have any legal ties to the business, outside of being married to me. That made it hard for anyone to connect her to anything when that money disappeared." He was quiet for a moment. "It wouldn't surprise me to find out she and Mickey were up to something again. Maybe even have this woman promoted so she'd be the one holding the keys if something did go down again. She'd get the blame, the same way I did."

"Are you saying Mickey and your wife are the ones who stole from the company?"

After a brief pause, Ryan said, "I have no proof of anything. But I know it wasn't me."

Chapter 22

Jeffrey was out on his front porch when I pulled into his driveway. He stared down at me and said, "You decide to take me up on my offer?"

I ignored his question and walked toward him without an answer. "You know what, Jeffrey? I don't believe a man cheating on his wife is enough of a reason to kill her." I looked around his property, and the perfectly landscaped yard, not to mention the St. Johns just a few hundred feet from his back door. "I realize Sarah had a pretty sizable life insurance policy. But I don't get the feeling that's something you would've needed." I took another step closer and stood watching him from just below the bottom step. "But by you offering me money to stop investigating your own wife's death..."

"I didn't say it was to stop investigating her death."

"No?"

"All I asked was that you leave Emma alone." He looked down at the floor of his porch then looked toward me again. "Well, I offered you money to leave us *both* alone."

"I don't see how that's two different things," I said. "I can't exactly continue investigating if I'm to completely ignore the fact the victim's husband was having an affair. Throw in the fact you were coincidentally at Emma's when you got the call about Sarah..."

Jeffrey shook his head, put his hands on his sides. "I was at the office."

"If you're going to keep lying... I do this for a living, you know. And I have a way of getting people to talk to me, even when it's someone you'd hope would cover up for you. Let's just say it's one of my few assets."

"I already admitted I was having an affair. That's not news. So don't go trying to credit yourself for being Sherlock Holmes."

I laughed and turned from him, looking around the yard. "I know plenty more about you than you realize. Same goes for Emma."

"What's that supposed to mean?"

"Everyone has a secret. If you think you know everything there is to know about Emma, you're mistaken."

Jeffrey dropped his arms by his side. "Of course I don't know everything about her. But that doesn't mean—"

"See this?" I pointed to what had become a scar just over my eye.

He squinted his eyes behind his glasses and looked down at me from the top step. He nodded. "What happened?"

"You know the person who did this. He showed up on my boat and attacked me while I was half asleep. And, like you, this person also wanted me to leave Emma alone. Except, he didn't offer me money. He offered me his fists."

Jeffrey said, "I hope you don't think I had something to do with it."

"There's no way you had anything to do with it. But you know him. And so does your girlfriend. In fact, Emma knows him quite well." I let that hang for a moment, then dragged Jeffrey along a bit more.

He appeared frustrated. "Why don't you tell me what the hell you're talking about?"

I said, "You really want to know? Okay." I waited, pausing for a brief moment. "You're not the only person in Emma's life."

Jeffrey's mouth hung open. He stared down at me. "You mean, she's..."

I said, "So, if your plan was to get rid of your wife so you could enjoy your young mistress for the rest of your life, those plans might not be as solid as you'd hoped."

Jeffrey's chest moved in-and-out, his breathing growing heavy. "Why should I believe you?"

"You don't have to believe me," I said. "I'm just telling you this because you may want to rethink offering money to protect someone who may not be as faithful to you as you'd hoped."

He paused, like he was thinking. "Was it Bruce? Bruce Rose?"

I was surprised he threw the name out like that. "What makes you say that?"

"Well, it's something I wondered about," he said. "But I saw him earlier, and he had stitches in his head. I asked him about it, and he said it was an accident. He said he'd walked into a steel beam."

I shook my head. "Close. But it wasn't exactly a steel beam." I looked down at the cuts and bruises on my knuckles.

Jeffrey closed his eyes. "How do you know? About Bruce and Emma?"

"What I'm telling you is if you're dreaming of a future with Emma, maybe you should think about it a little longer."

He held onto the column at the top of the stairs and looked toward the floor before raising his gaze. "So, what do you want from me?"

"Well, I understand Sarah also knew Bruce Rose?"

Jeffrey nodded. "He built the building for Hendrick Logistics. Sarah was involved in the project, at least the financial side of things."

"What about Kelly?"

"What *about* her?"

"What was her involvement with Bruce Rose?"

Jeffrey appeared to ponder for a moment. "Sarah had mentioned one time she thought there was something suspicious about Kelly and Bruce. But she didn't elaborate."

"You mean, an affair of some sort?"

Jeffrey shrugged. "I don't think so. She never gave me any specifics."

"And you never asked her about it?"

Jeffrey shrugged. "At the time, I didn't see how it had anything to do with me. The conversations Sarah and I had over the past year were few and far between."

"Did you ever wonder if Sarah was unfaithful?"

Jeffrey gave me a look and slowly shook his head. "Nothing I'm aware of."

"What about Mickey and Sarah? Was their relationship strictly business?"

Jeffrey nodded. "Yes, I believe so. Unless you think—"

"No," I said, "I'm just asking. I know he spoke very highly of her."

"Sarah always worked hard."

· · · ●·●·●· · ·

Billy stood behind the bar and poured a glass of Jack Daniels in front of me. He leaned with his hands on the bar and looked back and forth from me to Alex. "How's the case going?"

I shook my head and leaned back in the stool. I folded my arms at my chest. "I've never been so far away from having an answer in my life."

Three young men walked into the restaurant and sat at the other end of the bar.

Billy put up his finger. "I'll be right back."

I stared down at the young men…I'd say early twenties if even a day over twenty-one. I turned to Alex. "We need to talk to Wyatt about his parents." I yelled out to Billy at the other end of the bar. "Billy, is Jake in the back?"

He turned to me and nodded, then walked through the swinging door and into the kitchen.

A couple of moments later Jake walked through, right behind Billy and toward me and Alex. He stopped and poured himself a soda from the gun then came over and leaned on the bar between us.

"Billy said you wanted to talk to me?"

I sipped my Jack. "Have you heard from Wyatt Jenner?"

"I've been meaning to give him a call. I haven't talked to him since we were at his house."

"No?"

"He's been at school."

Alex and I exchanged a look.

"You knew him when he was younger, right?"

Jake nodded. "Since first grade."

"What was his relationship like with his mother? Were they close?"

He nodded, but with somewhat of a shrug. "I guess so. I don't know if they were as close the last couple of years. She went back to work, and he lived at school."

"Had their relationship changed?"

Jake didn't answer right away. He glanced at Alex then shifted his eyes back to me. "I really don't know." He paused. "Does this have to do with her accident?"

I said, "It does. I never really got a chance to talk to him. And he seemed to be handling things pretty well when we saw him at his house."

Jake looked down into his glass, quiet for a moment. "Are you asking because you think he might've had something to do with it? Because that would be crazy. Wyatt would never..."

"No, I have no reason to suspect her own son had anything to do with her death. But, I would like to talk to him again."

I grabbed a cocktail napkin and took a pen from in front of Alex. I looked up at Jake. "You mind giving me his number?"

Jake reached in his pocket and pulled out his phone. He read me Wyatt's number. "He'll be home from school this weekend, you know."

"I thought you said you hadn't talked to him."

Jake stared back at me, perhaps offended I'd questioned him the way I had. "He posted it in one of our groups online." Jake pointed with his thumb over his shoulder, toward the kitchen. "I have to get back in there, before someone messes something up."

I nodded and forced out a smile. "Thanks, Jake. Appreciate your help."

Alex flipped through a pile of papers in front of her then turned to me. "You did make it sound like you thought Wyatt was hiding something, the way you said he seemed to be doing well." She gave a slight tilt to her head. "You don't really think he had anything to do with it, do you?"

I shook my head. "He was away at school then. But hopefully he'll be open to talking to us. We just have to keep in mind he's going to do what he can to protect his father. So we'll need to be careful."

Chapter 23

I was back at Friendship Park to meet a woman who had worked for Hendrick Logistics prior to Sarah being hired. She'd owned her own dog walking business, so I recognized her right away when she walked toward me with three leashed dogs, pulling her along.

Without a free hand, she smiled and introduced herself as Roni. "I didn't know Sarah at all, but I was sorry to hear what happened."

We started along the walkway and I told her my name. I handed her my card. "So how long did you work for Mickey Hendrick?"

She looked down at my card, but had trouble holding it steady with the dogs trying to take Roni for a walk. "Almost two years."

"And you worked in the same department as Sarah?"

She nodded. "She actually took over my job." She looked down at the dogs. "Things weren't going so well for me." She smiled. "I made one of those crazy mid-life decisions and started a dog walking business."

One of the dogs tugged at the leash and pulled Roni off the path so he could lift his leg up on the side of a tree.

"Why do you say things weren't going well?"

She shrugged. "They'd let a few people go, and being the one in the accounting department, I saw the numbers." She looked down toward the ground. "I don't know where the money was going. There seemed to be plenty of work coming in. But sometimes we'd have trouble paying our vendors." She pulled the dogs along. "But they're still in business, so maybe things got turned around?"

"They have a new building, so I assume so."

She nodded. "They started it a few months after I left."

"Don't you find that odd?" I said. "I mean, I don't know much about that world, but if you're telling me they went from struggling to pay their bills to putting up a new office building a few months later..."

She shrugged. "I honestly don't know much about it at all. But I did find it strange. Although I understand Mr. Hendrick got a good deal on the property." She looked around them before she turned back to me. "I know another builder who bid on the job. He said something was rigged."

"In what way?"

"I'd just heard the company that got the work was going to get it all along. But they brought in other bidders anyway."

We walked for another few moments, both of us quiet along the way.

I said, "Did you get along with Kelly Swift?"

She laughed. "Kelly was part of the reason I left."

"Why's that?"

Roni shrugged. "We never got along very well. Kelly was in charge of our department. And she always made sure everyone knew she was in charge. If you ever questioned a charge or payment to a vendor that didn't make sense, she'd rip it from your hand without explanation. She'd just say she'd take care of it herself."

"But I understand Kelly and Sarah got along," I said. "Good friends, from what I've been told."

Roni stared back at me. "Let me guess, that's what Kelly told you?" She pulled the dogs' leashes toward her. "Kelly's what you'd consider passive aggressive. And anyone with a little sense could see right through her plastic smile."

· · · · ● · ● · · ·

Horns blew and tires squealed. Bruce Rose drove his Ford F-350 across oncoming traffic from the parking lot of the hotel where his construction company had been working.

Knowing he'd recognize my Jeep, I borrowed Billy's Lexus to follow him. I pulled out behind the F-350, following him onto 115. He headed toward Mathews Bridge, moving at a high speed across the bridge and over the St. Johns.

I stayed back to avoid being noticed, but turned just a few cars behind him onto University.

Bruce pulled his truck into an apartment complex called Congdon Apartments. It was the kind of place I'd normally avoid, especially at night.

The F-350 turned around the side of one of the buildings and a man walked up to his window on the driver's side.

I thought I'd done a good job staying unnoticed. But I had a feeling I was wrong when the man standing outside the truck's window turned and looked right at me. I was far enough back, but I could also see Bruce's eyes coming at me through his side view mirror.

I slouched down in the seat and wondered how he could know it was me. Unless he knew I'd been behind him the whole time, or had someone follow me earlier. Maybe even back when I'd picked up Billy's car.

I did my best to stay low, but there was a knock on the window on the passenger-side. And the first thing I saw, besides the man behind it, was the barrel of a gun. The muzzle was pressed up against the glass and pointed right at me. I turned and looked toward Bruce and his truck, but he was gone.

But the man outside the passenger window hadn't moved, his gun still pointed my way.

After Alex was shot, she gave me one of her Glocks. The problem was, it was in the glove box on the other side of the car. It was closer to the man outside the passenger-side door than it was to me.

There was no chance I'd be able to reach for it. Not unless I wanted to see if whoever was holding the gun pointed at me was going to pull the trigger.

The man tapped the barrel against the window and leaned down to look at me from outside. "Open the door." he said, his voice muffled behind the glass.

I stared at him, not sure exactly what to do. If I took a chance and reached for the gun, I'd get shot. If I tried to take off, well, I'd probably still get shot. But not at such close range. So that was a positive.

But before I had a chance to do anything, the man who had stood outside Bruce Rose's truck was outside my door. Like his friend, he had a gun in his hand with the muzzle no more than a foot away from my face, on the other side of the window.

I held my hands up in front of me, showed them both I was unarmed, then unlocked the door. I pushed the door open and stepped out. But before I could say a word, something hard cracked against the back of my head. I fell out of the car and dropped to my knees, looking up at the man standing over me. Then it happened again. I felt the same crack over the back of my head and fell face down onto the pavement.

Chapter 24

I woke up tied to a wooden kitchen chair with my hands behind my back. I squeezed my eyes tight and tried to clear the blur. My head throbbed on the inside and burned on the outside. I looked down at the blood on my shirt.

There was nothing else in the room but me and the chair. It was dark, but light slipped in through the blinds from the outside. There were two doors, one slightly ajar. The other closed tight.

I listened for a moment. I was pretty sure I was inside someone's apartment. Although it was dark, my eyes adjusted and I could see the construction-beige carpet and plain white walls. "Hello?" I said.

But nobody answered.

A door opened and closed somewhere outside the room and I heard a man's voice. I couldn't quite make out what he was saying. I wasn't even sure it was English. But then the voice grew louder and the door swung open.

Two men entered the room. One reached for the switch and flipped on the light. They both wore ski masks over their faces. One was tall and thin and looked to be mostly skin and bone. The other man was about a foot shorter, but twice as thick. The mask barely fit over his whole head…the fat part under his chin uncovered.

The tall, skinny man had a cigarette in his hand. He smoked it through the hole in the mouth of the mask.

The shorter one turned to his friend. "Do you have to smoke that in here?" He waved his hand through the smoke hanging in the air in front of him.

The tall one walked out of the room without a word, but came back a moment later without his cigarette. He stepped closer to me and stared without a word.

I looked back and forth between the two men. "So, what's this all about?" I said. My head pounded and I looked around the room. "You two live here?" I gave them a nod with my chin. "Roommates?"

The two exchanged a look then the tall one stepped toward me. Without a warning he threw a swift punch, square into my jaw. My head whipped to the side and my chin turned over my shoulder. I'd hoped to soften the blow. But it hurt like hell.

I closed my eyes. I thought maybe if I didn't see the next one coming, maybe it would hurt less.

But that didn't help. He threw another punch that again landed on my jaw.

He still hadn't said a word.

I cleared my throat. "Are you going to just keep throwing punches, or will you at least tell me the point of all this is? I know you're friends with Bruce Rose. What's the matter, he can't fight his own battles?"

The tall and skinny one hit me again. I felt the warmth of my own blood drip from my mouth and down my chin.

But this time, the man spoke. "Where's the key?"

I hadn't heard that one. "What key?"

The short and stocky one stepped forward. "We know she hired you to help find the—"

The tall one elbowed his friend then slapped him in the back of the head. "Shut your mouth," he said.

"Find the *what*?" I said. "And who hired me? I have no idea what the hell you're talking about?" I looked from one man to the other.

The tall one gave his friend a nod and the short and stocky man stepped toward me with his fist closed tight. He caught me right in the jaw.

And I thought the tall guy hit hard.

"Now," the tall one said with his hand extended, his palm open. "I want the key."

I turned my head and spit blood down on the carpet. "I get the feeling you don't believe me. But I'm telling you the truth; I don't have a key. I don't know anything about a key." I tried to work my hands behind the chair, hoping to at least get my hands free. But the rope's knot was tight. "Why not explain a little more about this key, maybe help jog my memory. You hit me pretty hard out there. Maybe the memory's a little foggy."

The tall one turned without saying a word and left the room. But he came back a moment later with what looked like a taser in his hand. "Maybe this'll clear your memory." He stepped forward and stretched his arm toward me with the taser in his hand. His boney forearm was covered in tattoos, one of a cross. A date ran through it vertically.

"Hey, that's a nice tattoo," I said.

His eyes shifted down to admire his own tattoo with the taser just a few inches from my chest.

I slammed my feet down into the floor and threw myself forward. I drove my shoulder into his chin.

He stumbled backward then hunched forward, reaching for his bloody face.

I spun around and shattered the legs of the chair I was tied to across his head. Broken slivers of wood exploded all over the room. He dropped face down to the floor.

I had already loosened the rope on my hands, and once I smashed the chair I was able to free myself.

The short, stocky one charged toward the taser on the floor and tried to charge me with it.

But I threw myself into him and drove my elbow toward his face. With a quick move on his part, I barely made contact. He threw a punch and knocked me down to the floor next to his friend

I reached for a splintered leg from the chair and drove the sharp end into the back of his leg.

He screamed in pain and dropped the taser. He fell to the floor and tried with both hands to pull the foot-long piece of broken chair from his bloody thigh.

I picked up the taser and shoved it into his neck. His body jolted and shook and he turned to his back. I ran from the room and tried to remove the rope and tangled pieces of wood from my arms and legs. I hurried through the dark, empty apartment and past the kitchen where the only thing on the counter was a paper plate filled with half-smoked cigarette butts.

I made it out to the parking lot—still somewhat dazed—and spotted Billy's Lexus. It was right where I'd left it.

I ran across the lot and reached into my pockets for the keys. But they were empty. The car door was open, so I reached my hand around the steering column and felt for the ignition. The keys weren't there, either. My phone wasn't on the seat where I'd left it. I reached for the glove box but it was empty. The Glock was gone.

I heard voices come from the building. I looked and saw the two men running toward me. The tall one ran ahead, blood coming down his face. The short one had such a limp, he looked like Quasimodo running under the streetlights.

I closed the car door and ran for the street. I was unarmed, and not about to try and take them both on.

It was fight or flight.

I chose flight.

I heard the pop of gunshots. I kept my head low and ran past the other cars in the lot and out onto Arlington River Drive. I had trouble catching my breath, but moved as fast as I could and continued along the expressway.

I finally slowed my pace, then stopped. I looked back, and knew I'd lost them both.

Chapter 25

It must have been midnight when I knocked on Alex's door. Her lights were off inside. Raz pounced on the window from the inside with his big paws up on the sill. He had a ferocious bark, but I knew he had no bite.

A light came on inside, upstairs from Alex's bedroom. I looked through the window panes on the door and the light came on over the porch.

Alex opened the door, Barefoot with nothing on but shorts and a t-shirt. She had her gun raised in front of her but lowered it when she saw it was me.

Her eyes widened. "What the hell happened?" She studied my face, clearly with much more damage than the last time she saw me. She reached out and pulled me by the arm and led me inside.

We sat down on her couch.

I said, "I followed Bruce Rose. Next thing I knew I was tied up inside an apartment. Two goons tried to beat the crap out of me."

She said, "*Tried* to beat the crap out of you? Looks like they did a pretty good job." She got up and walked into the kitchen, came back a moment later with a bag of ice and held it against my head. "Where were you?"

"An apartment complex, not too far from here. In fact, I walked here."

Alex walked out of the room and came back with a towel, then sat down next to me and cleaned the dried blood from my face.

"I don't know which cuts are from tonight or which ones you already had."

I nodded. "I'm kind of getting sick of being beat-up."

"So was Bruce Rose one of the men who—"

"No," I said. "It was two other guys I'd never seen before. He was outside the apartments. But I know he led me there on purpose. He was gone when I woke up tied to a chair."

"Woke up?"

"Yeah, got whacked pretty hard on the head. I was knocked out."

She said, "Did you get an apartment number?"

"No. I ran so fast to get out of there, I didn't even really have a chance to look."

Alex was quiet for a moment. "Don't you think we should go to the cops? Especially since you know Bruce Rose was involved?"

I reached for my stiff jaw. "They asked me about a key."

"A key to *what*?"

I shrugged. "I have no idea. I didn't stick around long enough to finish the conversation."

Alex got up from the couch. "You want a drink?"

I cracked a smile. "You read my mind."

I sat holding the ice on my head while Alex went into the kitchen for a drink. I thought about the key, and knew I had to figure out what it was all about.

Alex came back with a short glass filled halfway with Jack Daniels. She placed it down on the coffee table.

I picked it up and took a sip, but the cuts inside my mouth made it burn. "You know how we both wondered if Sarah really wanted to hire us because Jeffrey was cheating on her? Or if there was something else to it?"

Alex sat down on the couch again and nodded.

I said, "It was too obvious Jeffrey was cheating. There had to have been more to it. And now I wonder if whatever key these men were looking for has something to do with why she really wanted to hire us."

· · · · · · ● · · · ·

I spent the night in Alex's guest room and we both headed for the apartment building where I had my incident, to put it lightly, not even ten hours earlier.

We stepped out of Alex's Jeep and I opened the door to the Lexus with the spare set of keys I picked up from Billy. I nodded toward one of the buildings. "I was pretty disoriented when I left. I wish I paid more attention, because I have no idea which building I came out of."

We walked together across the lot. I looked back and forth from one building to the next. There were four buildings in the entire complex, and they all looked the same.

I pointed toward the one in the middle. "Maybe it's this one."

Alex grabbed my arm. "Wait," she said. "You sure it's smart for us to just walk in there?"

I had a snub-nosed .38 tucked in my pants. And Alex was armed. So I wasn't worried. I didn't love carrying a gun, but I sure felt safer when I had one. "Let's at least see if anybody's there, if I can even figure out which apartment it was."

"Why don't we just go see Bruce Rose at the hotel he's building?"

"Maybe I'm wrong," I said, "But I don't think he's looking to have a friendly conversation with me."

We stood underneath the building on the first floor of the garden-style apartments and looked at several different doors.

I jumped when a door opened behind us. An old couple walked out. They both used canes to help them walk. They stopped when they saw us.

"Good morning," I said.

Without a word, the old man grabbed the woman by the arm and hurried her away from us, toward the parking lot. But the old woman stopped and looked right at me. She said, "Are you okay?"

I pointed with my finger in my chest. "Me?"

She nodded. "You look like you've had an accident."

Before I could answer, the old man pulled her again by her arm and they disappeared around the corner.

Alex let out a slight laugh. "She's right," she said. "You're a mess. I'd be startled too if I walked out of my home to see a sight like that."

I looked at all the doors and shook my head. "This isn't the right building. I'm sure they all look the same, but..." I put my hands on my hips and looked out toward the parking lot. "I remember brushing against a palmetto tree when I ran out to the parking lot. I grabbed onto it, thought I was going to hit the ground." I walked out from where we stood and into the lot. I looked from one building to the next.

A palmetto tree caught my eye and I walked toward it. I stepped closer, and noticed a spot of red on the bark.

I was pretty sure it was my own blood.

I turned to Alex. "This is it." I walked past the stairs toward the ground-floor apartments. I looked at all the doors then glanced back at Alex. "This is it."

She pulled her Glock from her holster.

I raised the .38 in front of me.

We both approached the door with our guns drawn. I knocked and turned my ear against the door to listen. But I heard nothing.

Alex stepped to the side with her gun up. I knocked again.

"You sure this is the place?" she said.

I reached for the knob and turned it. But I didn't expect the door to be unlocked.

It was.

I pushed it open and we both stepped over the threshold. We had our guns drawn. The fluorescent light in the kitchen was on, but it flickered. There was blood dried on the floor. The paper plate with the smashed cigarette butts was still on the counter. The place stunk like old smoke.

As I took another step I kicked a piece of wood across the linoleum. I turned to her. "I don't think there's anyone here."

Alex walked past me and pushed open one of the doors off the small living room area. Right away, she said, "Henry? Get in here..."

I stepped into the room behind her. She turned from inside the room and looked me right in the eye then nodded toward the far corner of the room, just under the covered window.

A man was flat on his back on the floor. His legs were straight out, his arms by his side. His face was covered in blood. He had a gunshot hole, right between his eyes.

I froze in disbelief then turned to Alex. "It's Bruce Rose."

Chapter 26

Detective Mike Stone showed up at the apartment complex with another half-dozen uniformed officers behind him. He lit a cigarette and stared at me. Alex and I stood just outside the apartment building where Bruce Rose had been killed.

Mike said, "I should lock you up, just for being here." He kept his eyes on me, his face a bit twisted. He squinted his eyes. "What the hell happened to you, anyway?" He pointed with his thumb over his shoulder. "If it had anything to do with what happened in that apartment, you'd better start talking."

I shook my head. "I tripped on the dock."

Mike opened his mouth to talk but before he could, an officer walked toward us and yelled out Mike's name.

The officer wore blue rubber gloves and held out a broken leg from the chair I was tied to the night before. "Look at this."

Mike looked close at the leg without touching it. The jagged edge of the broken leg was stained in blood. "Where'd you find it?"

The officer turned and looked toward the lot. "Over there, underneath a car."

"I assume it fits that broken chair we found inside?"

The officer nodded, put the chair leg in a clear plastic bag and sealed it closed. He turned and walked back toward the lot.

Mike took a drag of his cigarette and looked off for a moment without saying a word, although I knew something was about to come out of his mouth.

Mike was the type of cop who liked to add a little extra drama to the job. I had no doubt he spent most nights watching cop shows...made sure he had the right look.

Alex gave me a look then turned to Mike. "You mind if we take off?"

He shifted his eyes back to Alex. "Are you serious?" He took another drag and blew the smoke right past me. "Neither one of you've given me even a hint of a believable explanation of why you were here in the first place. And you're not leaving until I have an answer." He turned to me.

I said, "I already told you, we came here looking for someone else."

Mike made that face again, the one where his lips got twisted like he just bit something sour. He scratched his head with the same hand holding his cigarette, his thick finger wrapped around it like a pool cue. "And like I already told you, you're full of shit." He glanced at Alex. "Don't let this clown prevent you from cooperating with me, Alex. I know you always do the right thing."

She said, "If you're asking if either of us had anything to do with what happened, or if we have any idea why he's dead..." She shook her head. "The answer to both questions is, no. As Henry said, we had a reason to be here, but that wasn't what we'd expected to find. If we had anything valuable to share, you know I'd tell you."

Mike looked off and slowly shook his head. He sighed. The cigarette hung from his mouth. "He's corrupted you, Alex. You can't just withhold information about—"

Mike stopped mid-sentence and the old couple Alex and I saw earlier walked up to us. The old woman stared at me for a moment then pointed her finger in my face. "My husband was right. He said you looked like a hoodlum."

The old man stood behind his wife and turned to Mike. "We saw this man outside our apartment this morning. Then we realized he was the same man who ran across this parking lot last night." He turned to his wife. "I told you we should've called the sheriff's office."

Without looking at him I could feel Mike's eyes, laser-focused right on me. "I knew you were lying, Walsh. So now we're going to do things *my* way." Mike called for one of the officers. He wrapped his big hand around my arm. "Take Mr. Walsh into custody."

Alex stepped in front of Mike, "You have it all wrong. Henry didn't have anything to do with this. That's the truth."

Mike put his hand up toward Alex. "Save it for the judge, or I'll take you in with him."

Two officers stepped toward me and slapped handcuffs on my wrists. One of them read me my rights. They pulled me away and I looked back at Mike. "You can't just arrest me because two old people said they saw me."

Mike had a sly smile on his face. "Actually, I can."

· · · ● · ● · · · ·

Mike walked in the empty room at the station where they had me down in a chair, cuffed to a long table. He sat across from me then reached over with a key he took from his pocket. He removed the handcuffs from my wrists.

"I've been here two hours," I said, "and you still haven't told me what you're charging me with." I shook my head. "You can't do this, Mike. It's not even legal, I'll just—"

"I can do what I want. And if you'd learn to shut your mouth for a minute." He folded his arms and leaned back in the chair.

"You go ahead and tell me what the hell's going on, and maybe there won't be any charges."

I laughed. "What you mean to say is you know I've done nothing wrong and you hope I'll admit to something so you don't look like such a fool?"

Mike leaned forward on the table and folded his hands down in front of him. "You tell me, right now, what you know about Bruce Rose. And what you were doing at that apartment."

I started to give him my best stare. But I couldn't do it. I turned away, looked off for a moment while I thought about what I should tell him. Or if I should talk at all. I knew he could only hold me for so long until he'd have to come up with a solid reason for arresting me in the first place.

I knew Mike's games well. But I wasn't in any position to compromise. So I sat, quiet, for a few moments.

"Okay," I said. "I'll admit I was there last night."

"Tell me something I don't know."

"I followed Bruce from the place he works. Bruce is—or was—the super for the general contractor building that new hotel downtown. I followed him to those apartments where he met a man outside at his truck. Next thing I know, I had a gun pointed at me from outside the car. Bruce took off, then the other man came up, stood outside my door. I'd barely stepped out, was hit in the head and got knocked out cold. Woke up tied to a chair in the same apartment where Bruce's body was found."

Mike shook his head and rubbed his face with his big hands. "Jesus Christ, Walsh. So how am I supposed to believe you didn't shoot Rose yourself?"

"Because I didn't. Those two guys beat the shit out of me while I was tied to that chair."

"You mean the chair we found busted up, all around that apartment? And the piece with the blood on it?"

I nodded. "I escaped, knocked one of 'em with the back of the chair. The other one came at me and I grabbed the broken leg, stuck it right into his thigh."

"So Bruce Rose wasn't there, after you were tied to the chair?"

"No. Like I said, he took off when the two men surrounded my car."

"Your Lexus?"

"Yeah. It's not actually mine. It's Billy's. I used it thinking Bruce wouldn't recognize me."

Mike stared back at me. "So then why'd you and Alex go back there this morning? To find these two men?"

"Yes. I was *not* expecting to see Rose there."

Mike got up from the table and rubbed the stubble on his face. "I'd like to believe you, Henry. I hope you didn't kill Bruce Rose. But—"

"Jesus, Mike. I didn't kill him. I'm telling you the truth."

"Then why'd you force me to take you here before you'd open your mouth? You could've made this a lot easier on both of us." He sat down again and stared at me from across the table. "But you still haven't told me the whole story. Why were you following Bruce Rose in the first place?"

Chapter 27

ALEX PICKED ME UP from the station and drove back to Billy's Place. As soon as we sat down at the bar, her phone rang. "It's Mike," she said. She got up and took the call outside.

A moment later she came back to the bar. "He said there's still not enough to re-open Sarah's accident case, but there's of course a homicide investigation into Bruce Rose's death."

I shook my head. "Didn't he listen to a word I said? I knew it. I wasted my time telling him just about everything. Now he'll use what I told him, just to make sure we get stonewalled at every turn. That son-of-a-bitch. He wouldn't take my lead unless I wrapped it up for him in a way that he could take all the credit."

Alex shrugged. "He said he went through the report and all the files. There's just not enough there to reopen it."

"And you believe that?"

She turned from me and looked straight ahead at the bar.

I said, "I told him what we noticed at the scene. You really think he went out to the creek in the short time since I walked out of his illegal arrest?"

"He said with the storms that came through the last couple of nights, it was impossible to use muddied car tracks to make any definitive determination."

"He held me for four hours and he ignored whatever I told him."

Alex straightened out in her seat. "It's not just Mike," she said. "You know how they are. And the Sheriff's not about to take a lead from a private investigator."

"Why not?"

Alex didn't say a word. She didn't really have an answer. "Maybe if you and Mike could work together without trying to prove each other wrong all the time..."

"Are you kidding?" I said. And I was asking a serious question. But I knew it was time to let it go. Mike wasn't going to do me any favors, and I knew we were on our own. Which wasn't such a bad thing.

· · · · · · · · · ·

I picked up Melinda after calling her to ask her if she knew anything about a key that might've had something to do with Sarah. And, without hesitation, she told me about a safe deposit box Sarah rented from Amelia Bank and Trust, in Fernandina Beach. She'd given Melinda the second key but didn't exactly explain why.

I hadn't realized Amelia Bank and Trust was one of the few left on Amelia Island that still offered safe deposit boxes. I never had one myself. I guess I never had anything valuable enough to need one. So it was news to me that most people had moved to using private companies to store their valuables. Banks had gotten out of the safe deposit business.

We pulled into the Amelia Bank and Trust parking lot. I said, "Is this Sarah's regular bank?"

Melinda turned to me and shrugged. "I don't know why she'd come all the way over here if it wasn't."

We stepped from the Jeep and headed for the bank's entrance.

I said, "She didn't tell you anything about what it was for? Or why she'd want you to have the second key?"

"Other than asking me to keep it somewhere safe, she didn't say what was inside. I just assumed... I don't know. What do most people use safe deposit boxes for?"

I pulled open the glass door. "I don't know. A will? Savings bonds?"

We explained to one of the tellers why we were there, and were told to sit in the small waiting area with four leather chairs and a TV up on the wall that showed low-budget local commercials without the volume on.

A young man in a suit approached us with an older woman about three times his age by his side. "Right this way," he said.

We walked down a hall past a handful of occupied offices and through double-glass doors, then through another solid door the young man opened with a combination he typed on a keypad. The door opened automatically and we followed the two into a vault filled with brass-plated drawers and doors. Each was numbered with three digits.

The woman took the key from Melinda and turned one of two locks on the drawer-face with the number 486. The lock clicked and she removed the drawer, then placed it on the table in the middle of the vault.

The young man stood behind the woman. She glanced at him with a nod and he looked at Melinda. "If there's anything else you need, please don't hesitate to ask." They both walked out the secured door.

I glanced around at the cameras on the ceiling in each corner of the vault.

Melinda removed the cover on the box on the counter in front of us and gave me a quick glance. We both leaned forward and looked inside.

There was a nine-by-twelve, manilla envelope folded in half inside the box. But that was it.

Melinda removed it and appeared hesitant to see what was inside. She pulled open the sealed top, then reached her hand inside. She pulled out a short stack of papers.

"What is it?" I said.

Melinda looked down at the papers. She looked me in the eye then handed them over. "Invoices, sent to Hendrick Logistics."

I looked down and flipped through the papers. "They're from a company called A.M.A. Freight, out of Georgia."

Melinda looked in the box. "Why would Sarah have invoices from work stuffed in a safe deposit box?"

"And you're sure she never said a word to you about any of this? She just gave you that key, and—"

Melinda narrowed her eyes. "You think I'm lying to you?"

"No, that's not what I mean. But, I wish she'd at least explained to you why she'd want you to be so careful with a key to a safe deposit box filled with invoices."

Melinda looked inside the safe deposit box and pulled out a smaller white envelope. She tore it open and reached inside, came out with another key. She held it up to me without saying a word.

I took it from her and looked at the numbers etched on the side. "I pulled out my keys and compared it to the key to my post office box. They were nearly identical. "I could be wrong, but I'd say it's to a post office box."

Chapter 28

ALEX WAS ALREADY WAITING for us when Melinda and I drove into the post office parking lot. I got out and walked toward her, handed her the key but before I could say a word, she took it from my hand and headed for the entrance.

I walked back to the Jeep and leaned against the front fender.

Melinda leaned her head outside. "So who does Alex know inside?'

"An old friend of her father's, from up in DC. Used to work at the main post office. Her father was a detective in Virginia."

"And he can just look at the key, tell her where it's from?"

"I guess he'll match the serial numbers etched on the side."

"So anyone can just go in there with a key and get the PO box number?"

I straightened myself off the fender and shook my head. "No, not at all. Helps to know the right people. And Alex knows just about everyone." I glanced up at the door then looked at my watch. "Do you have to get back to work?"

She shook her head. "No, not today. I took the rest of the day off. I have a lot of time coming. I haven't had a vacation in two years. But after everything that's happened, I've been rethinking my life. I'm not sure trying to break through that glass ceiling is as important as I thought it was, just so I can spend more of my life at a desk." She smiled. "I like the way *you* live."

"I thought you liked your job?"

She didn't answer. Her eyes moved across the parking lot then she turned back to me. Our eyes locked for a moment.

The doors to the post office slid open and Alex walked toward us with a piece of paper in her hand. "The post office for this PO box is up in Kingsland, Georgia. Right over the line." She handed me the key and the piece of paper.

I looked at the name and address on the paper. "Mary Cisco?" I stepped toward the passenger side of the Jeep and reached into the glove box.

My hand brushed up against Melinda's leg and she moved it out of the way.

"Sorry," I said. I grabbed the envelope we took from the bank and removed one of the invoices. I looked at the address on the top. "This matches the address on the invoice from A.M.A. Freight."

Melinda looked back and forth from me to Alex. "What does that mean?"

"It means A.M.A. Freight's mailing address is a PO Box. And somehow Sarah has the key. I turned to Alex. "Ready for a trip to the Georgia line."

Alex took the invoice from my hand. "Is that all there is? No street address?"

I looked down at one of the other invoices. I shook my head. "What kind of legitimate trucking company wouldn't have a street address on their invoices?"

"Maybe it's a small business? Some guy with a few trucks in his backyard."

I nodded and pointed to the name on the invoice. "And who the hell is Mary Cisco?"

• • • • • • • • • • •

Alex was already at her desk when I got back to the office after I'd dropped Melinda off at her condo. "Got a phone number," she said, her eyes on her computer screen.

I walked back to my desk. "Phone number to what? A.M.A. Freight?"

"Yup. But I called and it just rang and rang. Nobody answered. Not even voicemail."

"Did you find anyone named Mary Cisco?"

Alex looked up at me and shook her head. "None in Georgia. At least that I was able to locate."

I got up and poured myself a cup of coffee, then sat back at my desk.

Alex wasn't saying much, her eyes back on her laptop.

I had a feeling something was bothering her. But I had no idea what it could've been. I had to ask. "Is everything all right?"

She ignored me for a couple of moments, but finally looked across the office and stared right at me. She leaned back in her chair. "Well, I've been doing a lot of thinking."

I raised my cup of coffee to her. "That's why you're here. You're always thinking." I smiled, but didn't get the same in return.

She stared back, the look on her face serious as death. "Maybe you were right."

I was nothing short of confused, and had no idea where she was going. "I'd like to think I'm right at least once in a while. I get lucky sometimes." I put my cup down on the desk and folded my arms, waited for Alex to give me a clue as to where she was going to take the conversation.

Alex pushed her chair out from under her desk, put one foot up next to her laptop. She stared up at the ceiling with her hands behind her head, her elbows out wide. "What I mean is, maybe you were right...when you said you felt something was wrong. Or just off. Off about our business. About us. About this case."

I had a lump in my throat, but tried not to swallow. I didn't know if I should play dumb or if we should both just get it all out into the open, right then and there.

Alex said, "I feel like there's more friction between us lately."

"Friction?"

"I know you're going to think I'm crazy." She looked down at her desk. "I'm not even sure I should tell you this..." Her eyes came back up toward mine. "It's the way you look at Melinda."

"What?" I shook my head. "She's a client."

Alex folded her arms. "I'm just afraid, I don't know. It's just not very professional to—"

"You're way off base, Alex. The way I *look* at her? I'm not even sure what you mean by that."

She said, "Don't patronize me."

I threw my hands up. "This is crazy. Where is this coming from?" I thought for a moment, then held back a smile. "Oh my... That's it! You're jealous!"

"*I am not!*" she said.

"No? Then what is it? Because this is crazy. You're attacking me for not being professional? That couldn't be any further from the truth."

Alex closed her eyes and took a deep breath. "Okay, I'm sorry I said that." She stood up. "Maybe it's because of what you were saying the other night, out on the pier. How so much has changed between us, that we've gotten to a point where it's all business."

I said, "Isn't that how you said it should be?"

She walked to the window and looked out into the darkness over the St. Johns.

I went and stood next to her and we both stared through the glass, neither saying a word.

Alex reached down and grabbed my hand then turned to me. She leaned into me and kissed me on the cheek. Then, on the lips. We wrapped our arms around each other and kissed.

The door swung open from the back stairs and Billy walked in.

He covered his eyes with his arm up in front of his face, turning away. "*Whoa!*"

Alex and I let go of each other and walked back to our desks.

Billy turned back to us. "So, how long have you two been keeping this little secret from me?" He put his hands on his hips.

Neither of us answered.

He said, "Okay, well, I guess it's none of my business. Sorry for barging in, but I just came up to tell you someone was here earlier looking for you."

I said, "Does this *someone* have a name?"

Billy nodded. "It was Mickey Hendrick."

Chapter 29

ALEX AND I WERE on the dock next to my boat when I noticed a black Mercedes pull into the parking lot. Parked just a few spots down from my boat, I watched Mickey Hendrick step from the car.

He walked toward us. "Henry? I'm glad you're here. I've been looking for you."

"What can I do for you?"

He looked around, although the marina was quiet with very few people out on the docks in the warm sun. "I know we didn't get off to a good start the other day."

"Okay?"

He stepped onto the dock and stood in front of me next to my boat. "Is there somewhere we can talk?"

I shrugged. "Why not right here?" I looked around at the other boats. "Nobody's around today."

He glanced at Alex, then shifted his gaze back to me. "Just the two of us?"

I said, "Alex is a licensed investigator and partner in my business. Anything you have to say to me, you'll have to say to her."

He looked around some more. "Okay, but is there somewhere we can go? Something more private? I know there's nobody around, but..."

I said, "How about we go below and have a drink?"

Mickey waved me off. "I don't drink. But if it'll give us some privacy..."

He followed me and Alex up onto my boat and down to the cabin below.

"Sorry about the mess," I said, moving the mail and magazines from the counter. I pulled a stool away from the wall. "Have a seat."

He had an odd, soured look on his face, looking over at my bed. "Is this where you live? All the time?"

I said, "Your closet's probably bigger than this." I smiled, "But it's easy to clean."

Both Mickey and Alex looked at the pile of clothes on my bed.

I opened the refrigerator and pulled out a bottle of beer. I needed a drink. I held the bottle out to Mickey. "You sure you don't want one?"

He again waved me off. "No, thank you."

I held the same bottle toward Alex but she shook me off, too. I cracked the top then took a sip and nodded toward Mickey. "Whenever you're ready. I'm all ears."

"I again want to apologize for the way I acted toward you." He looked down toward the counter. "I've been under quite a bit of pressure. And things haven't been so easy after what happened."

"I assume you mean at work?" I said.

"I already told you, Sarah did a lot for us." He cracked a slight smile. "You know, she actually saved the business. She really helped turn things around. Found some holes where we were losing money."

"Yeah?" I said. "Like *how*?"

Mickey shrugged. "I don't know exactly what she found." He looked off for a moment, toward the small window over my bed. "I know it ruffled some feathers, but she really did deserve that promotion."

I looked down at my watch. "Mickey, what is it you wanted to talk about?"

He looked at Alex, then back to me before his eyes went back down to the counter where he picked at a piece of tile with his finger. He looked up at me. "Did Sarah tell you anything about me?"

I thought for a moment. "You mean, for instance, that she knew you were stealing money from your own company?"

Mickey's eyes sprung wide open. "Stealing money from my own company?" He cocked his head. "I have no idea what you're talking about. Is that what she told you?"

I shook my head. "She knew something was going on, Mickey. And you might as well come clean and tell me what Sarah found. Because I'm afraid she got herself caught up in some kind of a mess."

Mickey shook his head. His eyes shifted back and forth from me to Alex. "I am the CEO of my company. I built that place myself from the ground, after my first company almost ruined me. But you think I would steal from my own company? What exactly would I get out of that?" He started for the ladder, his face red as a beet. He looked at Alex and pointed at me with his thumb. "You believe this guy?"

I'm sure Alex knew what I was up to, throwing something we knew little about at Mickey. I was doing nothing more than hoping to get him to admit to something we had no proof he'd done.

"Okay," I said. "Then how about you tell me who Mary Cisco is?"

He snarled his lip. "Who?"

"Mary Cisco. With A.M.A. Freight?"

He shrugged and shook his head. "I've honestly never heard the name." He scratched his head, one hand still up on the ladder. "A.M.A. *what? Freight?*"

"You paid them hundreds of thousands of dollars over the past year. We have invoices that show the amounts that've been paid."

Mickey continued to shake his head. His eyes stayed down toward the floor. "We work with hundreds of vendors, Henry. Truckers…freight companies…auditors…" He shook his head. "I certainly don't know every vendor we've ever paid. I mean, it's not like we're running some local flower shop, writing checks as deliveries come in. We have over two hundred employees."

I waited for him to stop talking.

But he continued. "And, you know, hundreds of thousands of dollars may sound like a lot, but that's peanuts compared to some of the bigger companies we work with. I'm paying out millions a year to some of them."

"So your company pays hundreds of thousands of dollars to a vendor you've never heard of?"

He stared back at me for a moment without saying a word, then scrunched his face. "So who is this person, Mary Cisco?"

"Well, if you're not going to tell me who she is," I said, "Alex and I are going to go find out."

He stepped toward the counter and leaned with his hands down, his arms spread wide from his shoulders. He turned his head to look at me. "You have to believe me. I've done nothing wrong. I... I'll look into this freight company for you, if you'd like. Maybe I can get you some answers."

"How about, for now, you go ahead and tell us why you came here looking for me."

Mickey sat down on the stool I'd left for him. He put his short legs up on the lowest bar, had his hands flat on his knees. He looked right at Alex. "I love my wife, you know. I really do. But, sometimes when you're in a position like I am, I guess you could say things happen." He looked down into his lap. "Things that of course *shouldn't* happen, but they do. We all make mistakes, right?"

I wasn't sure how long it was going to take him to get to the point, so I thought I'd come right out and ask him the question I needed to ask. "Mickey, did you kill Sarah?"

His eyes opened wide, his eyebrows raised. "Me? No way. Never. Never even in a million years." He looked back and forth from Alex to me. "Sarah and I..." He stopped. "She was carrying my baby."

I was in the middle of sipping my beer and spit half of what was in my mouth on the floor. "Jesus Christ!" I said. "What do you mean she was carrying your baby?" I wiped my chin with the back of my hand and gave Alex a quick look.

Her eyes were wide open, as was her mouth.

Mickey stood from the stool and walked toward the sink in the galley. With his back to us he scratched his head, then turned. "Of course, having a baby with Sarah would have ruined my marriage. But I didn't care. I mean, it's not that I didn't care. Like I said, I love my wife." He looked at me. "I really do. But—and I know this sounds strange—I couldn't have been more thrilled when Sarah told me the news."

Alex stared back at Mickey. "You were *thrilled*?" She turned and gave me a look.

I just shrugged.

A tear came down Mickey's cheek. "My wife and I tried for years to have a baby. It almost destroyed our marriage." He looked down toward the floor. "We both blamed each other."

"Before you continue," I said, "I know I already asked you this but now I'm not so sure exactly where you're going with this news." I sipped my beer, but knew I needed something a little stronger. I wished I hadn't smashed my only bottle of Jack on Bruce Rose's head. "Mickey, I'm going to ask you one more time. Are you telling us this because you killed Sarah?"

Without a second of hesitation he shook his head. "God, no. Never!" He paused, his eyes on mine. "I grew up with five brothers and three sisters. Not having kids of my own was never even a thought. Everyone in my family has kids, but me."

Alex took a step closer to Mickey. "So, you purposely got Sarah pregnant?"

"On purpose?" He shook his head. "Of course not. It was a mistake. I told you that. I simply made a mistake. But, as I said, I was thrilled at the thought of having a child. But I wasn't going to leave my wife. I couldn't. I didn't love Sarah. And she didn't love me. But she was carrying my child, and—"

"What makes you so sure it was yours?" I said.

"She told me she hadn't been with anyone else. Not even that poor excuse-of-a-husband. I believed her when she told me they hadn't slept together in almost a year." He wiped the tear from his cheek and again sat down on the stool. He looked toward the floor. "My baby died in that accident with Sarah."

I looked toward Alex. "Nothing came up in the autopsy?"

Alex glanced at me and shook her head, then turned to Mickey. "Who else knows about this?"

Mickey shrugged. "I can't imagine anybody knows. I certainly didn't tell anyone."

I said, "What about Jeffrey?"

"I can't imagine she told him, although she knew at some point she'd have to. She knew it would've ruined her marriage for good, as if either one of them would have cared."

The three of us were quiet for a couple of moments.

Mickey looked at his watch and turned and glanced toward the ladder. "So, I need to get going in a moment." He looked back toward me and Alex. "What do I need to give you to keep this all quiet?"

I walked to my refrigerator and pulled out another bottle of beer. "You mean your affair with Sarah?"

"Well, it wasn't even an affair. We were only together one time."

Alex and I both had our eyes on him, waiting for him to finish.

"But I hope you'll keep this quiet. Just tell me whatever you need from me. Any amount of money. Whatever it'll take."

I said, "If you want to pay us to keep quiet, then why'd you tell us in the first place?"

"I'm telling you because I don't want you to think I would have ever done anything to hurt Sarah. I don't want you to think I'm a suspect."

I narrowed my eyes. "Mickey, I can't think of anyone who would have more of a motive than a man who got a woman pregnant and needs to ensure his wife wouldn't find out."

He shook his head. "But why else would I tell you?"

I leaned with my hands on the counter across from him. "How about if I make you a promise. If I find any connection whatsoever between you and what happened to Sarah... Your wife getting word about your affair—or whatever you want to call it—will be the least of your problems."

Chapter 30

WE PASSED THE SIGN for Kingsland, Georgia and I turned to Alex. "I imagine you have to go through a lot of trouble to rent a PO Box using a fake name or business."

Alex had her eyes on the road. "I'm not sure it's even possible."

"Anything's possible," I said. "Especially when you're raking in checks worth hundreds of thousands of dollars; you have enough to take care of a few postal workers, make things a little easier for you."

Alex was finally able to get the physical address attached to the PO Box. So before we went to the post office we searched for a building or a home with the physical address she'd found.

I reached for the radio and turned up the volume.

Alex gave me a look. "What's this?"

"The Bill Evans Trio."

"Since when did you start listening to this kind of music?"

I smiled and kept my eyes on the road. "See, maybe we don't know each other as well as we thought." I shrugged. "This music helps me think." I could feel her watching me.

She said, "You've never played the piano, have you?"

"When I was younger I did. But it's been a long time." I looked down at Alex's hand. The thought crossed my mind to reach for it. But ever since we kissed in the office, we'd both acted as if nothing ever happened.

Maybe that was the best thing to do.

....

We were a few miles from the Georgia line, still on 17, and turned off onto Highway 40.

Alex had her eyes on her phone again. "The GPS is spotty. I'm not getting any directions. But I think it's off here, somewhere." She looked toward the road and at the last second pointed toward the windshield and said, "Go right!"

I cut the wheel, almost taking the Jeep up on two wheels. That was one of the problems with the older model Jeeps. They weren't made for sharp or sudden turns.

The farther we drove down the road, the more sinkholes I had to avoid. Within a half-mile, the aged, cracked asphalt turned to dirt and gravel.

Alex held one hand up on the roll-bar, her other hand gripping the dashboard.

The road split. A large wooden sign on the road was painted with white, faded numbers that were hard to read. Arrows pointed right and left.

"Go left," Alex said.

I turned on the road, which quickly became more of an overgrown throughway than anything else. There were tire tracks that cut through the tall grass. We continued ahead as the Jeep bounced up and down with each dip in the earth.

After another few hundred yards we were mostly surrounded by trees, with tall grass and mud along the road. A mobile home was within view up ahead, with a big yard and a lot of trees surrounding it.

"That's it," Alex said. "Number six-four-nine."

I turned the wheel and we parked on the grass. I looked toward the home's narrow, aluminum door. A maroon Buick LeSabre with faded paint and rust covering the bottom of the doors was parked over a patch of dirt where the grass hadn't grown. Next to it was an old aluminum lawn chair with the same green webbing like the ones I kept at my boat.

Alex stepped from the Jeep and nodded toward the chair. "Is that yours?"

"Different color green," I said.

I stepped onto the makeshift cinder block step in front of the aluminum door. I listened for a moment and heard sounds, like they were coming from a TV. I knocked and waited.

Alex had her hand on the holster she wore under her shirt.

The sound from the TV stopped. I backed from the step and looked at a window a few feet from the door when I thought I saw a curtain move.

I knocked again.

The inside door opened. An old woman, paste-like white with dirty gray hair tied up on her head, stood behind the broken screen. She had a look to her I knew looked familiar.

I turned and glanced at Alex. The look on her face was as if she'd seen a ghost.

The woman had a look to her eyes like nothing I'd ever seen. They seemed to glow.

"Ma'am, my name's Henry Walsh." I nodded my head toward Alex. "This is Alex. We're here because this address seems to be associated with a PO Box owned by a trucking company called A.M.A. Freight." I looked around the yard. "I don't see any trucks in the area, but I'm wondering if by chance you might be able to help us out?"

The old lady still hadn't said a word, but her gaze shifted from me to Alex.

She started to close the door and Alex grabbed my arm.

"It's her," she said.

But before she could, I pulled open the screen door and stuck my foot over the threshold, stopping the door from closing. "Ma'am?"

The woman pushed on the door from the other side, but I didn't move my foot.

Alex said, "Did you see her eyes? It's her. From that Dodge Durango."

The pressure eased on my foot and I pushed the door open. "Hello? Ma'am?"

I looked into the darkness inside the home and didn't know where the woman had gone.

But then she stepped out from a room with a double-barrel shotgun, lifted it and fired a shot, just as Alex and I both dove out of the way.

We ran around the side of the trailer and another shot was fired. This time she blew the bark off the side of a tree no more than six feet from where we'd stopped.

I turned the corner of the home and tripped on what looked like a makeshift grave with a crooked wooden cross sticking out of the ground.

Alex pulled her Glock from her holster. "I'd hate to have to use this on her."

"Now's not the time to worry about granny," I said.

We leaned with our backs pressed against the side of the woman's home, out of view from the front. But a window opened just over our heads and the shotgun's barrel poked out of it.

The old woman yelled, "I should've taken care of you when I had the chance!" She fired another shot into the ground at our feet.

We went around back, where there was a small shed twenty yards away from where we were. There was a truck or an SUV parked behind the shed and covered with a blue, nylon tarp.

"You ready?" I said.

Alex gave me a nod and we both ran as fast as we could toward the shed.

But the woman fired another shot and hit the side shed.

Alex and I ran for a wood pile along the edge of the property.

As soon as we dove over the top, an engine roared. The tail lights on the vehicle behind the shed came on. Before we could make a move, the tarp flew off. Underneath was the green Dodge Durango with the dark tinted windows.

It Durango took off, rocks and grass and dirt kicking up all around it. A gunshot fired from the vehicle, and another from inside the trailer.

"Stay down!" I yelled. As if Alex needed my instruction.

The green Dodge drove around to the front of the trailer. A horn blew and we could see the old lady run toward it with the barrel of her gun pointed right at us. She stopped, pumped once and took another shot in our direction.

The bark on a tree behind us blew up, wood pulp dropping on our heads.

I raised my eyes up over the pile and watched the old lady jump into the passenger side of the Durango. It drove ahead and was out of our view, but two more shots were fired.

Alex and I jumped to our feet and ran to the side of the trailer. I stuck my head around the corner toward the front, but it was too late.

The old lady and whoever was in that Durango were long gone.

I looked over at the Jeep and saw I had two flat tires. "Shit," I said. "That's not good."

Alex looked out toward the so-called road. "That was them. That old lady shot me." She looked at me and shook her head. "This is unbelievable."

I walked to the Jeep and reached inside for my phone. I looked back at Alex. "You have a signal?"

She looked down at her screen and shook her head. "Nothing."

Chapter 31

I WALKED AHEAD OF Alex with my gun raised and stepped through the front door of the trailer. I stepped into the kitchen. The place smelled like fried food and cats, although I didn't see any cats.

To the left was a living area with a small TV and an antenna hung from a nail on the wall. There were three glasses with ice inside on top of a coffee table. I picked one up and sniffed inside. "Bourbon," I said. I reached down and picked up an empty box of Winchester Shells. I noticed two wooden chairs under the window. "I could be wrong, but those chairs look like what I was tied to. Although I can't imagine why they'd take a chair all the way down from Georgia, just so they could tie me to it."

Alex looked around the kitchen. "Doesn't look like much of a trucking company, does it?"

I walked past her and stepped into a bedroom with a double bed and a single side table next to it. The top of a tall dresser was covered with framed pictures. I pulled open the dresser drawers but didn't see much inside. I lifted the neatly-folded clothes but didn't find much of anything underneath.

I looked at the photographs on top. They all appeared to be older photographs and all of the same little girl. I pulled down one of them and turned to Alex walking in behind me. "Look at this," I said.

Alex took it from my hand then studied the photo. She shrugged and handed it back to me. "You know her?"

I looked at the photo. "You don't see it? Picture that face, maybe twenty years older."

Alex shrugged. "I give up."

I took a moment, wondering if I was trying too hard to get my mind to see what I maybe didn't see. But I knew I was right. "If that little girl isn't Emma Buckman, then it's certainly someone related to her."

Alex took the photo from my hand again and studied it some more. She looked at me. "I guess I see it. But..."

"It's her. Look at it." I grabbed another photo of the same girl but maybe a little older. I pointed to the photo. "If I'm right, then what the hell is her relationship to the old lady?"

"Does this mean Emma Buckman's behind all of this? Behind Sarah's murder?"

I placed the photo back on top of the dresser but didn't answer Alex's question. I looked around. "Let's see what else we can find in here, see if we can make some connection's to A.M.A. Freight." I had almost forgotten I had two flat tires and one spare. And two cell phones without a half of a signal between them. I walked from the bedroom and used the landline phone hung on the wall in the kitchen.

Billy answered on the first ring. "Where are you?"

"In the middle of nowhere, just over the Georgia line." I told him I had two flat tires.

"How'd you get two flat tires?"

"An old woman with a double-barrel shotgun in her hands. Luckily she didn't have a very good shot, although we're pretty sure she's the same person who shot Alex the other day."

"The old lady shot Alex?"

"Looks that way. But listen. I hate to ask, but we need a ride. We're pretty much stuck."

Billy didn't hesitate a moment. "Text me the address. I'll leave right away."

"Actually, neither of us have a signal on our phones."

"Where are you calling from?"

"We're inside the old lady's trailer."

· · · ● · ● · · · ·

I hated to have to leave the Jeep behind at the house but we couldn't hang around, either. So Alex and I left on foot and walked side-by-side through the overgrown weeds and grass along the road.

Alex said, "Can all of this really be connected to Sarah's death?"

I hesitated a moment before I answered. "I wish I knew. But right now we have no idea why she had those invoices, and why she has the key to a PO Box owned by a freight company we're not even sure exists."

We walked in silence for the next hundred yards or so. The only sounds around us came from the birds and a few screaming hawks.

Every few steps I'd look back over my shoulder, worried the old lady and whoever was behind the wheel with her would come looking for us. We were sitting ducks.

I stopped and wiped the sweat from my forehead with the back of my arm. "What if Sarah is actually the one behind all of this? How do we know she wasn't stealing from Hendrick? We don't know a thing about her, do we? And what if that key was meant for Melinda from the start? Finally gets to that PO box and finds a stack of cash or checks or whatever's in there."

Alex said, "Maybe we should have gone to the post office before we went to the house."

We continued our walk and kept quiet for the next two-and-a-half miles until we finally made it to the post office parking lot.

We walked to the front door of the building and a horn blew.

Billy pulled in and parked behind us. He put down his window. "Need a lift?"

I nodded but turned back to the door and held up the key. "As soon as I see what's inside this PO Box." I pulled open the glass door and walked toward the small room off the lobby. There were three walls covered in various sized post office boxes.

I moved my eyes up and down the numbers and stopped on the one I was looking for: 4738. I stuck the key inside and turned it once, counter-clockwise. I looked inside the box and pulled out a handful of envelopes postmarked as recent as two months ago. There were eight in total, one sent every Monday of every week.

The return address was Hendrick Logistics, sent from Jacksonville.

I walked outside toward Alex and Billy waiting by his Lexus.

I handed the envelopes to Alex then tore one open myself. I removed a check and stared at it for a moment. I held it up to Alex and Billy. "It's made out to A.M.A. Freight for thirteen thousand dollars." I looked at the signature. "Signed by Kelly Swift."

I opened another one and pulled out another check, also signed by Kelly, made out to AMA. I held it up to Billy and Alex. "This one's for eight-thousand dollars."

Billy said, "Can you tell me what's going on here? Or you just want me to shut up and drive you home?"

"Well," I said, "for some reason Mickey was sending Sarah these checks. I don't know what A.M.A. Freight is or what her connection is to it. Or if the company even exists. It doesn't look like it. We still don't know if that old lady is Mary Cisco or not."

Alex said, "Do you think Kelly's involved with some kind of scheme?"

Billy had a confused look on his face. "Involved how?"

I had opened another envelope and looked up at Billy. "The old lady had pictures of a little girl in her bedroom. And I'm almost certain they were pictures of Emma Buckman, when she was a child."

"Emma Buckman? That's Sarah's husband's girlfriend, right?" Billy scratched his head. "And what about the dead guy from the apartment?" Billy said. "What's he got to do with all of this?"

"Bruce Rose?" I shrugged and shook my head at the same time. "I honestly have no idea. Not yet, anyway."

We all stepped into Billy's Lexus and took off onto the road.

Alex leaned forward from the back seat. "Those envelopes look like they'd been piling up long before Sarah was killed."

"Sorry to interrupt, but, did you say whoever shot at you was driving an old green Durango, with tinted windows?" I turned and saw Billy's eyes up in his rearview mirror.

I turned around and looked out the back window.

Alex did the same.

And all three of us saw them. Granny and her gang were right behind us.

The car in front of us had stopped and turned sideways. We had nowhere to go.

Chapter 32

I TURNED FROM THE passenger seat and watched the old lady walk from the Durango behind us, blocking the road. She had the double barrel shotgun by her side, and didn't move at all like an old lady, each step she took a long, exaggerated stride.

Two men followed behind her. Without a doubt, I knew they were the men who had tied me to the chair at the apartment. The tall skinny one held a gun in his hand. The short stocky one had a wooden baseball bat.

I turned back to Billy. "Either you have to get us past that car ahead of us, or we're going to have to go out there and fight."

Billy looked toward the car ahead of us, then turned and looked over his shoulder toward granny and the two men. He reached under his seat and came up with an old Ruger 9mm he'd had for as long as I'd known him.

"When was the last time you shot that thing?" I said.

"Took it to the range a couple of years ago." With a single nod, he said, "Don't worry, I can hit a target."

I looked back at the old lady and the two men. They had stopped walking toward us, and for some reason hadn't yet fired.

Although I had a feeling granny was itching to pull that trigger.

Billy turned around in his seat with the Ruger in his right hand. "The last thing I want to do is shoot an old lady, but..." He looked back at Alex. "You sure that's who shot you?"

Alex was slouched down in the back seat with the Glock in her hand. She stayed low, ready to come up firing.

Billy turned back toward the steering wheel and reached his hand down for the shifter. The engine was running, and he slapped it into reverse and slammed his foot down on the gas.

I turned in the passenger seat and saw the old lady and her boys dive out of the way to avoid being clipped by the rear-end of Billy's Lexus.

He ripped the steering wheel and spun the car around.

With his foot on the gas, Billy held the wheel with one hand—the other holding his Ruger—and tried to squeeze past the green Durango still blocking the street.

But there wasn't enough room. He smashed into the side of the Dodge and dropped his gun on the floor. He grabbed the wheel to maintain control of the Lexus.

Alex yelled "Look out!"

Billy tried to avoid a live oak but he clipped it once we were past the Durango. He tried to keep control but drove straight into a chain link fence at the entrance of an abandoned parking lot.

I turned in my seat and watched the old lady and her boys come to their feet and run back to their vehicle.

Billy cut the wheel hard and took us toward 40 West.

"They're coming!" I yelled, reaching down for Billy's Ruger on the floor next to his foot. I looked up at the sunroof and pushed the button to open it. With the Ruger in my hand, I stood on the passenger seat and stuck my head through the opening.

Both the Dodge and second vehicle were catching up.

Billy was going too fast for me to take aim, so I dropped the barrel a couple of degrees and shot at the grille. I pulled the trigger and fired a single shot. Steam came up from under the hood but the Durango didn't slow. They stayed right on our tail.

The skinny, tall man I recognized from the apartment hung outside the passenger window with a shotgun in his hands.

"Get down!" I yelled to Alex and Billy.

The man started to fire and sprayed bullets toward us. He blew out the rear window.

Alex was crouched down on the floor in back.

Billy ducked his head without taking the Lexus off the road. He yelled into the wind blowing around the inside of the car from what used to be the rear window. "Will you just shoot him!" Billy yelled over the sound from the wind. "Do you need me to come up and shoot that thing? Or are you going to just let them keep firing at us?"

Alex tugged at my shirt. "Will you get down before you get shot!"

But I didn't.

I stood up through the open sunroof again, and raised the 9mm toward the Dodge behind us. Even though the windshield was tinted, I could see it was the skinny man behind the wheel. I tried to aim, then pulled the trigger. The bullet ripped through the windshield but I wasn't sure if I'd hit him.

The Dodge crossed two lanes and smashed straight into the Jersey barrier along the side of the highway. The other car behind it kept driving and disappeared past us.

We slowed down and pulled off the road.

I pulled open the door and put one foot down on the ground. "I'm going to see which one of them knows what happened to Sarah."

Sirens could be heard coming toward us, but still off in the distance.

Alex pushed open the back door and stepped out next to me with her Glock still in her hand. She walked ahead of me along the breakdown lane and headed toward the smashed SUV. She got closer and had her Glock raised in front of her.

I ran to catch up to her. "Wait!"

I looked back and saw Billy step out of his car. He popped the lid on his trunk and came out with another gun in his hand. He hurried toward me and Alex.

Cars buzzed by us on the highway. The three of us walked side-by-side in the breakdown lane.

We approached the Durango, unsure who was dead or alive inside.

Three police vehicles came screaming around the corner. One car was from the Georgia State Patrol. The other two were Camden County Sheriff's vehicles.

The deputies from Camden stepped out with their guns drawn. The state patrolman walked toward them then turned to the Durango. He removed his weapon from his holster.

One of the two deputies walked past the Durango and pointed his gun toward the three of us. He yelled, "Drop your weapons!"

All at once, without a second of hesitation, we placed our guns down on the pavement and raised our hands up over their heads.

He yelled again, "Face-down on the ground! Hands behind your head."

I looked past the deputy and saw the patrol officer reach for the driver's side door on the Dodge. I yelled to him, "They're armed inside that Durango! Don't let that old lady fool you!"

I stayed down on the ground and tried to watch.

Two more vehicles arrived from the sheriff's office. Two deputies rushed to assist the others standing just outside the Durango with their guns still drawn.

The Durango's back door opened and the old lady stuck her head out. "Help him, he's hurt."

The officer opened the driver's side door and reached in to help the wounded driver. The tall skinny one stepped out with his hands up in the air. Blood came down his face. "I've been shot," he said, then dropped to the ground.

We were all handcuffed and thrown in the cruisers. I showed my private investigator's license and tried to tell our side of the story, but it went ignored. The deputy tucked my head down and guided me into the back seat of his cruiser. "That old lady shot Alex. And I'm sure if you trace these guns, you'll match them to a bullet left in a man named Bruce Rose, who was shot to death down in Jacksonville."

"We get down to the station, you can do all the talkin' you want," The young deputy slammed the door in my face then got in the front seat.

Alex leaned forward with her face against the steel grate. "Will you please at least contact Detective Mike Stone, with the Jacksonville Sheriff's Office?"

The deputy put the car in drive without a word.

Billy turned and tried to look out the rear window. "Where are they towing my car?"

"It'll be at the station on East Fourth. That's where it'll be."

"East Fourth?" I said. "East Fourth where?"

"Woodbine." The deputy removed his hat and placed it down next to him. "Camden County Headquarters."

Chapter 33

I GRIPPED THE BARS of our cell and tried to listen to the old lady and her short stocky friend in the cell next to us. She told the deputy her name was Mary Cisco, but I was sure that was a lie.

I heard the man whisper and the old lady told him to shut his trap.

There was a good chance the two were related.

Billy leaned forward on the bench at the back of our cell, his elbows down on his knees. "What's going to happen here?"

I turned to him, "I think once they realize we're the ones telling the truth here, we'll be freed."

Alex stood next to me and leaned on the bars with her arms folded at her chest. She looked back and forth along the empty hallway. "You say that like it's automatic."

"What's 'automatic?' "

She kept her eyes outside the cell. "That they'll suddenly realize we're the good guys."

The deputy walked through a door and stepped toward our jail cell.

"Excuse me," I said. "Is there any chance you happened to call Detective Mike Stone yet, with the Jacksonville Sheriff's Office?"

The deputy stared through the bars. He took a moment before he answered. "I spoke with him." He turned his eyes toward Alex. "He mentioned Mr. Walsh tends to drag you into trouble like this once in a while."

I pointed into my chest. "Me?"

The deputy walked away, in the direction of the cell with the old lady and the tall skinny man.

Billy got up from the bench. "How long can they legally keep us without pressing charges?"

Alex and I both turned to Billy but neither of us answered.

The deputy walked past us again and looked straight ahead. He headed for the door.

"Excuse me," I said. I pushed my face close to the opening between the bars.

He stopped with his hand on the doorknob then turned to me with a nod. "What?"

"What are the charges?"

He stared back at me. "Reckless driving, for one. Although that's a misdemeanor. Illegal discharge of a weapon. Firing a weapon on a state highway, well, that's a whole 'nother story. And if by chance that man you shot doesn't survive surgery, then I think you can guess what that would mean."

"You're kidding, right? I think the word you're looking for is called self defense. They shot at us, more than once. You see all the holes in Billy's Lexus? The rear window that just so happens to be missing?"

The deputy didn't say another word, pulled open the door and disappeared.

• • • • • • • • • •

The door opened and the voice I heard was *not* one I'd normally be happy to hear. But I was actually relieved when I saw Detective Stone walk through with the young deputies and Chief Deputy Enis Jackson.

The deputy stepped forward and slid his key in the jail cell's door.

Billy pushed past me. "Are we free?"

"Not quite," the deputy said.

I looked at the three men in front of us and stepped out of the cell with Alex and Billy. "What's that mean, 'not quite?' "

I turned and glanced back at the old lady in the cell adjacent to the one we were in, separated by a concrete wall.

She stared back at me with her creepy, green eyes.

Alex turned and whispered to Mike. "That old lady, I'm almost certain she's the one who shot me."

Mike stared down at Alex then looked over at me and Billy. "But you just drive into Georgia, act like a gang of vigilantes."

I laughed. "You see what they did to Billy's car? Looks like Swiss cheese. All we did was try to get away."

The Chief Deputy Jackson spoke up. "You broke into the woman's home. Isn't that correct?"

Alex and I both exchanged a look.

"We didn't break-in," I said. "The door was open. And that was only after she shot at us three or four different times."

Chief Deputy Jackson turned and walked through the door without another word, stopped and held it without looking back.

We followed him out of the holding area and into the same room they held us in before they decided to lock us in the cell.

Jackson sat at the end of the long table and gestured with his hand toward the other chairs. "Have a seat." He looked up at the young deputy in the doorway and gave him a nod. "I'll take it from here." We sat at the table and the deputy closed the door behind him. Chief Deputy Jackson turned to Mike. "Go ahead."

Mike looked at each of us from across the table, quiet for a couple of moments. He appeared to gather his thoughts, then stopped with his eyes on me. "Why don't you go ahead and start from the beginning." He glanced at Chief Deputy Jackson. "And Jackson has assured me, you leave anything out this time he'll be sure I won't have to worry about seeing you down in Jacksonville for a while." He turned his chin down and stared at me through the tops of his eyes. "You got that?" He turned to Alex. "I need to hear every detail. And I want the truth."

I said, "Then you'll help us?"

Mike glanced at the Chief Deputy again, then slowly nodded and shifted his eyes back to me. It was clear, even though they were from different states, this wasn't their first dance together.

"Well, to begin with, we didn't drive all the way up here to break into an old lady's mobile home." I thought for a moment, then looked across the table at Mike and the Chief Deputy. "I'm not so sure that old lady you have back there in that cell is Mary Cisco."

Chief Deputy Jackson leaned forward on the table. "What makes you say that?"

"Alex and I saw a photo at her home. I didn't realize it until I saw her up-close earlier but, in the photo, which had to've been twenty years old... She had a little girl on her lap. If I had to guess, that old lady is either the grandmother or aunt or...someone who is related to a young woman named Emma Buckman."

I went on to explain who Emma Buckman was, and her relationship to Jeffrey Jenner and how she was sleeping with Bruce Rose—the man who was killed in Jacksonville—and that I had no doubt she was the same person we saw in that photo as a little girl.

"Jeffrey Jenner?" Mike said. "Sarah Jenner's husband?" He leaned back in the chair and folded his arms, eyes squinted. "Didn't I make it clear that the case was closed."

I said, "Closed for the sheriff's office. Doesn't mean I can't keep asking questions, Mike. It's my legal right to do so." I shrugged. "And you can't just arrest me because you don't want me to prove the cops made a mistake."

Mike put up his hands, his palms out toward me. "Okay, we're not going to go into all of that right now. So why don't you just go ahead and tell me how all of this ties together. Please."

"If I'm right about that photo—that the little girl is Emma Buckman and the old lady is not Mary Cisco—then I can prove this all ties together. It will lead us to the person who killed Sarah Jenner."

Chapter 34

Jeffrey was out waiting for us in front of his house when Alex and I pulled into his driveway. I could tell right away he looked to be in shock. At least that's what I saw on his face. He stepped toward us. "Are... Are you sure it was her?"

"The old lady confessed. They have a cadaver dog in the back yard. And unless she's lying... Mary Cisco was her daughter, which makes her Emma's mother. They buried her behind the old lady's mobile home."

Jeffrey held his hand on the side of his face. "But, why?"

"We don't know the whole story, but allegedly Mickey Hendrick was making payments to Mary Cisco, through a shell company he'd set up for her when her husband, Emma's father, killed himself. He was an investor in the company Mickey started with Ryan Swift."

"Kelly's ex-husband?"

I nodded. "Emma's father lost all his money in that business. He gambled on Mickey and Ryan. And lost."

"I don't understand how..."

"I'll get there," I said with my hand up, my palm toward Jeffrey. "Mickey paid the wife, Mary Cisco—using her maiden name—weekly payments to make up for the money her husband had lost investing into Mickey's first company. But sometime after Mary Cisco died, they couldn't open the PO box where the checks were sent. But somehow they knew Sarah had the key."

Jeffrey looked confused, as was to be expected. "But, did someone really confess to killing Sarah?"

I shook my head. "Not yet."

He shook his head and looked past me, toward the road. "But what about Emma? Are you sure she was involved?"

"Not yet. The grandmother confessed to the scheme and hid the fact her daughter had died. But nothing else so far."

"But what would any of this have to do with Sarah's death?"

"That's why we need your help. We want you to get Emma to talk. I don't know if she'll confess, but..."

Jeffrey looked down toward the ground then eased himself down and sat on the bottom step from his porch. He kept his eyes down for a few moments then looked up at me and Alex. "I didn't want to admit this, but I was afraid all along Emma might have had something to do with it."

I started to speak then stopped and rubbed my hands up and down my face. "Then why didn't you say something? There are a lot of people who thought it was *you*, Jeffrey. Maybe if you'd mentioned it sooner."

He shrugged. "I guess, the morning I went to her apartment—when I got there—it was almost as if she'd just gotten home. She seemed to be out of breath. And wide awake."

Alex and I both exchanged a look.

"Jeffrey," I said, "I hope you're telling me the truth."

He nodded, and looked to have tears in his eyes. "I can't believe this. Just tell me...what do you need me to do?"

"Get Emma over here," I said. "And get her to talk."

· · • • • • • • · ·

Alex and Mike Stone stood next to me behind the cabana, just beyond the pool. We were no more than twenty feet from the patio where Jeffrey and Emma stood together in the darkness.

Emma looked around the patio and out toward the pool. "Why do you have the lights off out here?"

Jeffrey didn't answer.

"I can't stay long," she said.

They stood face-to-face and he reached for both of her hands. "Where are you going?"

"I have to meet someone a little later."

I watched Jeffrey and wondered if he remembered every-thing we'd told him to say. Although, even though he wasn't a person I'd like to hang and have a drink with, I felt he was smart enough to figure out what he should do.

"Emma," he said. "I know what happened."

Emma gave a slight tilt to her head. "What happened to *what*?"

"I know about your grandmother. I know what happened to your mother, and the money your family was getting from Mickey."

Emma went quiet, stared back at Jeffrey and took a step back, away from him. She shook her head. "I have no idea what you're talking about."

Jeffrey folded his arms. "I need you to tell me what hap-pened. Maybe I can help you. I need you to tell me how Sarah was involved in all of this."

Emma again shook her head and took another step back from Jeffrey. "If I knew what you were talking about, I would tell you. But I honestly have no idea. And you're starting to scare me." She turned and started for the door.

Jeffrey grabbed her by the arm and I looked at Mike, stand-ing next to me watching through the shrubs next to the cabana.

"Was Sarah onto your scheme? Is that why you killed her? The way you acted at your apartment that morning."

Emma ripped her arm from Jeffrey's grasp. "Are you crazy? What's wrong with you? The morning at my apartment? Are you kidding me? If you thought I had something to do with Sarah's death that morning, then why did you tell me you loved me, for the first time?" She stormed through the door and into the house. Jeffrey followed after her.

The front door slammed and the windows on the back of the house shook.

Jeffrey's voice echoed from somewhere around the front of his house. "Emma!"

A car's engine roared. Tires squealed.

We watched from where we were, saw Jeffrey through the windows, walking alone inside his house.

Mike looked back at me. "Good job, Walsh. Didn't you advise that moron on what to say to her?"

The three of us stepped out from behind the cabana and I said, "He didn't listen. He didn't say *anything* I told him to."

Alex said, "I don't know. I'm not sure I'd blame him. Maybe we got it wrong." She shrugged. "Maybe Emma has nothing to do with any of this, other than being related to the old lady?"

We walked past the pool and I looked down into the blue water, the light from the half moon reflecting off the top.

Chapter 35

BILLY STEPPED TOWARD ME and dropped two cubes into my glass then poured a good shot of Jack over the top. "So what are the charges?"

"Well, the old lady and the two nephews are being charged with conspiring murder, blackmail, mail fraud, and charges of attempted murder for shooting Alex. I believe there's an extortion charge thrown in there."

Alex sipped from her bottle of beer. "But there's nothing on Emma. She claims she knew nothing about any of it."

Billy leaned with his hands down on the bar. "You really think she's clean?"

I sipped my drink and looked back at Billy over the rim of my glass. "I don't know what to believe. If she is involved, she's done a good job of covering her tracks."

Billy cracked the top open on a small bottle of Perrier then took a sip. "And they're opening up the investigation into the accident?"

Alex leaned with her elbows on the bar. "The sheriff's office still won't bite on it being staged. But they are willing to go back and re-examine the records to confirm the cause of death. Mike said it's the best he could do."

"What does that do?" Billy said.

I shrugged. "It keeps the window open."

"But you don't have any other leads?"

I sighed, looked up at Billy then threw back most of what was in my glass. "Even Mickey Hendrick looks clean, other than admitting he'd made payments illegally through his company."

Billy said, "Isn't that a crime?"

I nodded. "I think they'll come down on him one way or another."

"And how'd she die? The old lady's daughter?"

"We don't know yet."

Alex said, "I still find it unbelievable Emma didn't know her mother was dead."

I looked up at Billy. "She said she hadn't spoken to her in over a year. They had some kind of falling out."

Billy scratched his head and squinted with a slight tilt to his head. "So Mickey Hendrick was sending this money to

Emma's mother because he felt guilty about the husband's suicide?"

"He lost every penny he had," I said. "Because he invested everything in Mickey's business."

Billy shook his head and turned to walk away. "No wonder why you couldn't figure this one out."

Alex leaned into me. "I still wish there was a way to prove whether or not Sarah was actually pregnant with Mickey's child."

I turned to her and shrugged. "But why would he make up such a story? Besides, he has the cleanest alibi out of everyone we suspected. His wife said he was home, left the house at six-fifteen. Security officer at his building saw him walk in the door at six-thirty, sharp."

Alex gave me a look then turned her eyes and stared straight ahead down the bar.

We both remained quiet for a few moments, sitting, watching Billy take care of the other customers at the bar.

"You know," I said, "What if Kelly had a reason to hide her involvement in all of this? Her signature was on the damn checks."

I thought for a moment. "Her signature was on all the checks. But, even so, her friends at the gym admitted she held up the aerobic class. She told the instructor to wait before she started because she thought Sarah was running late."

· · · ● · ● · ● · · ·

I drove Alex home and took her up on an offer to have a few more beers on her porch. It was still light out, although the sun had started to go down.

Alex sipped from the bottle in her hand and leaned forward in the chair. "What about Melinda?" she said. "Do you think it makes sense, Sarah would really give her a key and not tell her what it was for?"

I was about to sip my beer but stopped. "I don't believe Melinda had anything to hide. You don't hire a private investigator if you're hiding something. And, keep in mind Sarah didn't expect to die. At least not that we know of." I reached into the cooler for another beer.

Alex kept her eyes on me but took a moment before she spoke. "Well, let's hope they can get more out of the old lady and those two creeps."

I stood up from my seat and looked out from the porch. "What if Sarah had planned to tell me everything she knew. Maybe I could've met with her the night before, we wouldn't be grasping at straws." I turned to Alex. "I was the one who said I'd meet her the next morning."

Alex looked up at me from her chair, one leg tucked up under the other. "Don't start blaming yourself for something.

That's foolish." She sipped her beer. "We still have no idea if all she really wanted was for us to prove Jeffrey was cheating."

I leaned back against the railing and stared down at the floor without saying a word. I looked up. "I guess I'm glad we didn't take Melinda's money."

Alex's phone rang. She answered, "Nancy? Yes, it's a good time." She sat quiet with the phone up to her ear. "I'm glad to hear that." She was quiet and listened with a blank look on her face. She stood from her chair and brushed a strand of hair from her face with the same hand she held her bottle. She stood on the top step of the porch and looked in the other direction, then turned to me. She spoke into the phone. "Chlorine and Calcium Hypochlorite? Are you sure that's it?" She kept the phone up to her ear, shaking her head.

I knew by the look she had in her eyes we might've had something.

"Okay. Thank you. I can't tell you how much I appreciate your help on this. I owe you, big time." Alex tapped her phone and put it down on top of the railing.

"Who was that?" I said, "And what about Chlorine and Calcium Hypochlorite?"

Alex looked at me, but took a moment before she said anything. "That was Nancy, from the Medical Examiner's office." After a brief pause, she said, "You were right. Nobody analyzed the water removed from Sarah's lungs. She said it was simply overlooked, they've been so busy over there. But she went ahead and ran an analysis. Found Chlorine and Calcium Hypochlorite in Sarah's lungs."

"Isn't that what you'd find in a swimming pool?"

Alex stared back at me and didn't say a word. She didn't have to.

Chapter 36

Jake and Chloe pulled up next to me in the parking lot outside Billy's Place. Jeffrey and Sarah Jenner's son Wyatt stepped out of the passenger seat and stood in front of me and Alex.

Alex and I both straightened up off the hood of my Jeep.

"I know I haven't told you exactly what this is all about," I said. "But I appreciate you doing it."

Wyatt handed me the mason jar filled with water. "This is about my mother, isn't it?"

Alex and I both exchanged a look, then I gave Wyatt a nod, not wanting to say too much. "I'll tell you everything we know...as soon as we find out more." I looked at the jar in my hand. "Was your father home?"

Wyatt stared at me, maybe at a loss for words. He shook his head. "I waited until he was gone. I haven't even seen him since my mother's service."

I said, "You and your father don't get along?"

He shrugged. "You could say that. I know he'd cheated on my mother. We never had much of a relationship anyway." He shifted his gaze toward the jar. "Do you think he had something to do with my mother's death?"

I looked off, out toward the river behind the parking lot. "Why don't you let me do what we have to do with this water. Then you and I can talk. I promise I'll tell you everything I know."

Wyatt looked from me to Alex, nodded slowly, then turned and stepped back into Jake's car without another word.

· · · ● · ● · ● · · ·

It was late in the evening when Alex and I pulled up in front of Jeffrey's house. Mike was parked out in the road and stepped from his car and walked alongside me and Alex up the driveway.

We walked up the front steps and saw the door cracked open. Light came out from the inside.

I turned to Mike. "Why don't you let me go inside first?"

"For what?"

I shrugged. "Just trust me."

Mike gave Alex a look and I walked in by myself without looking back.

"Jeffrey? Are you here?"

He didn't answer, but I heard a noise come from the kitchen. I walked slowly down the hall then turned. Wyatt had a gun pointed at Jeffrey.

Jeffrey was down on his knees with his hands behind his head. He had tears coming down his face.

"Wyatt!" I said, "What the hell are you doing?"

He gave me a quick glance over his shoulder. "I know he killed her."

I reached out and put my hand on his shoulder. "Wyatt, don't do it." I looked back behind me. "We have someone from the sheriff's office here. Let us take care of this."

Jeffrey cried. "Jesus Christ, Wyatt! Listen to the man, will you? I didn't kill your mother. I swear I..."

"Shut up!" Wyatt yelled. He took another step closer to Jeffrey. He had the gun pointed right at his head, from no more than six feet away. "You never loved her. You never cared about anybody but yourself."

I stuck my head out into the hall and saw Mike and Alex step in through the front door. I nodded for them to come toward us. "Wyatt's here," I said. "He's got a gun."

Mike pulled his Glock from his holster and held it down by his side. He walked toward me.

"You don't need that," I said. "Not yet."

I turned to Jeffrey and Wyatt. "Wyatt, please. Let us take care of it. You don't want to have to deal with something like this for the rest of your life."

He gave me another quick look over his shoulder. "He killed her!" Tears came down his face. He turned back to Jeffrey. "She didn't deserve to die." His gun shook and he took another step closer to Jeffrey. "But YOU do!"

"I didn't kill her!" Jeffrey yelled with his eyes closed and his arms out in front of his face. He turned his head to the side and whimpered, his eyes still closed. "Please don't shoot me, Wyatt. I'm your father for Christ's sake."

Wyatt laughed. "You're not my father. I know the truth. I found the papers. You weren't man enough to make your own child."

I glanced at Alex and Mike.

Wyatt kept the gun pointed at Jeffrey, both hands wrapped tight around the grip. "You're nothing but a low-life. You're a liar."

My heart pounded. I was sure Wyatt was going to pull the trigger right then and there.

But Alex stepped past me. Her voice was calm. "Wyatt?" She reached for him. "Don't do it. Please." She put her hand on his arm and eased it down by his side.

I reached toward his gun and pulled it from his hand.

Alex had her arm over Wyatt's shoulder and walked with him past me and Mike and out of the kitchen.

I waited until I heard the front door open and close.

Jeffrey jumped to his feet and reached for a knife from a block on the counter. He started to step away. "You can't prove anything," he said. The whimpering expression he had on his face had changed to anger.

Mike had his gun up, pointed right at Jeffrey. "Put that knife down. Or I *will* shoot you."

Jeffrey didn't listen, had the knife up in front of him and stepped backward, slowly toward the doorway behind him.

"Why'd you do it, Jeffrey?" I said. "Why'd you kill your wife?"

He shook his head. His mouth moved, but words didn't come out. He took another step away from us.

Mike said, "I'm going to pull this trigger."

Jeffrey raised the knife over his head and threw it across the kitchen toward me and Mike. We both ducked and he ran the other way, through his house and out the back door.

Mike hadn't fired his gun. We both took off after Jeffrey and through the same doors Jeffrey had gone out of. We chased him across the patio and toward the pool. Mike ran after him and I cut around the other side. I ran at him head-on and he dropped his shoulder. He tried to run through me, but I wrapped my arms around him.

He struggled to get loose, but I held him tight until he lost his footing. I tossed him into the pool. He grabbed onto a pink flamingo float then swam across to the other side of the pool.

But Mike was there waiting for him with his gun pulled and pointed at Jeffrey. "Get up here now and get down on the ground."

Jeffrey swam away and stayed in the middle of the pool holding onto the float with both hands. His breathing was heavy and labored. He looked back and forth at me and Mike on either side of the pool.

I said, "There's nowhere for you to go, Jeffrey."

He didn't move right away, but after a few moments made his way to the ladder just below where I stood. He pulled himself up and sat on the edge of the pool, his feet in the water. He turned and looked up at me, and I wasn't sure if it was tears or pool water in his eyes. "Sara was pregnant. And there was no way I could've been the father."

I looked at Mike and he slipped his gun back into his holster. "You killed your wife because she was *pregnant*?" He took a cigarette from his pack and stuck it in his mouth.

Jeffrey looked across the pool toward Mike. "Like I said, it wasn't my child."

I said, "Sarah told you?"

Jeffrey looked up at me. "I found a photo from her ultrasound. And when I confronted her, she seemed like...she seemed relieved that I knew." He looked down toward the far end of the pool, toward the house. "We argued for a few minutes. I was so upset. But I didn't mean to. I... I pushed her. I'm telling you the truth when I say I don't even know exactly what happened. She didn't hit her head or anything, but..." His voice turned to a whisper. "When she fell into the pool, I watched her. I expected her to start to swim. Or do something. But she didn't. She didn't move at all. She never came out."

Mike walked over and stood next to me. We both looked down at Jeffrey before Mike pulled out his cuffs. He crouched down, lifted Jeffrey to his feet and read him his rights, then led Jeffrey to the house.

"Jeffrey," I said. "Did Emma have anything to do with any of this?"

He stopped and turned to me, hands cuffed behind his back. He paused, like he had to think about it, then shook his head. "No."

Chapter 37

ALEX AND I SAT out on the dock next to my boat with drinks in our hands. We watched Mickey Hendrick walk toward us from across the parking lot then onto the dock.

He said, "I hope I'm not bothering you?"

I looked up and shook my head. "Not at all."

Mickey stared down. "Would you mind?" He nodded toward the bottle of Jack Daniels under my chair. "I think I could use a drink."

I got up from my chair and onto the boat, grabbed Mickey a glass and gave him a good pour.

He took it from my hand and stared into the glass without taking a sip. I wasn't sure if he'd changed his mind.

Mickey turned and stepped toward the edge of the dock. "My wife left me." He looked out toward the river. "Of course, who can blame her?"

I looked into my glass. "Is that why you're here? Looking for sympathy?"

He turned to me, shaking his head. "You deserve the truth."

Alex stood from her chair and said to Mickey, "Just so we're all clear, we can't make any promises about keeping any secrets."

"I don't expect you to," he said. "In fact, I'm telling you tonight because I'm going to the sheriff's office in the morning. I don't know what'll happen to me, or if I've even committed any punishable crimes."

I reached up onto the boat and pulled down another chair, put it down across from the two chairs Alex and I had out on the dock. "Maybe we should sit." I nodded toward his glass. He hadn't even taken a sip. "You don't have to drink that if you don't want to. A man gives up drinking, it's usually not a pretty site when he falls off the wagon."

Mickey sat in the chair and finally took a sip. He seemed to keep it in his mouth before he swallowed, maybe adjusting to the sweet warmth of the whiskey. "If there's ever a time I should start drinking again..."

Alex and I both sat in our chairs. I reached over and filled her glass with wine, then topped mine with another splash of Jack.

"You two do this a lot?" Mickey said, looking around.

"Do what?" I said.

"Sit out here on the dock, enjoy your cocktails together along the St. Johns?" He looked off toward the water. "I know you're partners and, of course, it's none of my business, but—you ask me—you seem like you have a pretty good relationship. I don't know if you're together or not. I mean, outside of work, but..." He took another sip. "I'm just saying, it's not easy finding someone you like to be with all the time."

I didn't look at Alex. And neither of us responded.

I leaned forward, elbows resting on my knees. "Mickey, why don't you go ahead and tell us why you're here."

He threw back his head and finished his drink, then held out his glass. "Do you mind?"

I grabbed the bottle from under my chair and topped off his glass.

He said, "When the sheriff's office asked me about that key, I wasn't exactly honest with my answers. But I'm going to tell you why Sarah had it in the first place."

I took a deep breath and leaned back in my chair.

"First, let me just tell you about Bruce Rose." He sipped his drink. "His father was involved in my first business. As an investor."

"The business you had with Ryan Swift?" I said.

Mickey nodded. "Like the others who were willing to help us get started, he invested quite a bit of money in our little business. And, like everyone else, he lost a fair amount of money. Then, after he died—"

Alex said, "After *who* died? Bruce's father?"

"Yes. He had a heart attack. He was quite a big man, not very healthy to begin with." Mickey sipped his drink. "Well, I felt like I needed to take care of his son, Bruce. So I gave his company that project to build the new building for Hendrick Logistics. Problem was—at least for him—he was only an employee. It was a good position for a young man, but he really didn't make much money off of it. Probably got him a nice raise, but..." He looked toward the river. "Not so long ago, Bruce—the son—approached me and said I owed him money."

Alex said, "Why, because his father lost money?"

"That, and, well, Bruce found out I was paying Emma's mother, through A.M.A. Freight. So he thought he should have the same arrangement."

I said, "How'd he find out?"

"I thought maybe it was Emma Buckman. But, come to find out, it was Sarah. She knew he grew up in Kingsland, Georgia. So for some reason she asked him if he'd heard of A.M.A. Freight..." He gave a slight shrug of a shoulder. "She pretty much opened a whole can of worms."

"Why didn't Sarah ask *you*?"

Mickey sighed. "She had a feeling I was up to something illegal. And she didn't even want to mention it to Kelly. She was afraid she'd uncovered something bigger than it actually was. And Sarah and Bruce had gotten friendly, so—"

"Friendly? How friendly?" I said.

Mickey shook his head. "Oh, I don't think there was anything to it. They weren't romantic or anything. Not that I know of. But..."

"Can you tell us how Sarah ended up with that key?"

Mickey looked down, then lifted his eyes to mine. "Because I gave it to her. And, well, once word got around she'd hired a private investigator... We didn't know how much you actually knew. Or how soon until you'd find out."

I said, "So Bruce came after me because he thought Sarah gave me the key?"

"I told him it made no sense she'd give it to you," Mickey said. "But he didn't like to listen. The man could be a little too aggressive sometimes..."

I huffed out a slight laugh. "Yeah, I noticed." I got up from the chair. "Do you know why the brothers killed Bruce?"

Mickey shook his head. He looked up at me from the chair.

Alex stood up next to me and we both looked down at him.

I said, "So you still haven't said why Sarah had that key, or why she had those invoices stuffed in a safe deposit box."

Mickey got up from the chair and got up on his toes to see inside my boat. "Like I said, she thought I was up to no-good, copied those invoices. She figured out A.M.A. Freight was a shell company, but had no idea why. So she started asking around." He smiled. "She was like that. Liked to ask a lot of questions. I don't know how well you got to know her, but you would have liked her. She would've made a good investigator." He leaned with his hand up on my boat, the drink in his other hand. He took a sip. "In fact, the night she approached me about those invoices, I came clean with the whole story. It just happened to be the night we, well..."

"Christ, Mickey. You still haven't said how she ended up with that key." I looked down at his glass and wondered if he'd had enough.

He looked me in the eye. "She didn't believe my story. Not at first. So I gave it to her, told her if she went up there, she'd find all those checks."

"Did you tell the old lady and the two brothers Sarah had the key?"

"No! Why would I do that? But, I guess it's possible, maybe Sarah told Bruce. Or," he shrugged. "Maybe Emma really was involved. Who knows if Jeffrey..."

"Emma hasn't admitted to anything," I said. "And her grandmother sure wasn't going to throw her under the bus."

Alex sat back in the chair. She turned to Mickey. "But didn't the old lady already have the key?"

Mickey took a deep breath and let it all out with a heavy sigh. "See, I hadn't heard from Mary Cisco in a while. As I guess you already know, Mary is the old lady's daughter. And she was Emma's mother, although estranged. Mary had even stopped using her married name after the husband died."

I'd started to lose my patience with Mickey. "So then what happened with the damn key?"

"Like I said, it'd been at least a couple of months since I'd heard from Mary. She hadn't answered my calls. And the truth was, I didn't even know where she lived. She moved around. So I drove up to the post office in Kingsland. The woman behind the counter—the same woman who'd helped us set up the PO box for our so-called business—told me she hadn't seen Mary in a few months. She said two men had been coming in, taking the mail from the PO box. I had no idea who they were. So I went ahead and had the lock on the box changed."

"When was this?" I said.

He shrugged. "A couple of months ago. I figured if Mary couldn't get her checks, my phone would start ringing."

"But nobody ever called you?"

Mickey shook his head.

I said, "Why didn't you just stop sending the checks?"

"Because it would have raised too many questions at my company. Maybe even the IRS. Not to mention, Kelly Swift would've started asking questions."

I reached for my bottle from under the chair and topped off my drink. "Kelly didn't know A.M.A. Freight wasn't a real company?"

He shook his head. "She's oblivious to a lot of things I had to do to keep my company afloat. She just does her job...keeps her head down. I think she's happy that way."

I stared back at Mickey. "I'm still not clear why you gave Sarah that key."

Mickey held his glass in front of his mouth, about to take a sip but stopped. "Because she was carrying my baby. She'd have to be taken care of. The money was already going out the door, the business was already set up. I'd set her up, get her on a new account in Georgia so she wouldn't have to worry about money. Especially if she'd left Jeffrey." He handed me his empty glass. "I gotta get to my hotel." He looked toward the parking lot. "It's only a block away."

I said, "You're staying at a hotel?"

"Like I told you, my wife threw me out."

Chapter 38

Alex and I were out for coffee at Java Jazz by seven in the morning. Alex's phone rang and she got up from the table. "It's Mike," she said, and went outside to take the call.

The door opened and Melinda walked past Alex.

I gave her a wave. She came over and sat down in the seat across from me, where Alex had been sitting.

"Where's Alex going?" she said.

I sipped my coffee. "Just taking a call from Detective Stone, with the sheriff's office." I pointed toward the counter behind. "Can I get you a coffee? Or tea?"

She shook her head and looked at her watch. "I have a flight out in two hours."

"A flight? Where are you going?"

She smiled. "I quit my job. I don't know if I'm going to go the extreme and live on a boat, like you do, but I'm going to change the way I live."

"You make it sound like I live like a bum," I said.

"No, not at all. But you do what you love. And you live the way you want to live. I admire that." She reached into her purse and pulled out an envelope. She slid it across the table and looked me in the eye.

"What's this?" I picked it up and looked inside, then put it down and pushed it back across the table. "I told you, we weren't charging you anything, Melinda. I owed you that."

She shook her head. "That's foolish, Henry. You did what you said you would do. And you did it faster than you said it would take."

I felt my throat choke up and tried to hide my swallow. "But, you're the one who said it was Jeffrey from the start."

Melinda shrugged. "But for all the wrong reasons. *You* were the one who was right. You said you needed proof..."

Alex walked through the door with her phone in her hand. She sat in the chair next to me.

"Everything all right?" I said.

Alex nodded. "Emma Buckman was arrested for Bruce Rose's murder."

I felt my eyes open wide. "What? How did they—"

"The two older people we saw."

"The ones at the apartment," I said, "who said I looked like I was up to no good?"

Alex nodded. "They saw Emma leave the apartment early that morning. The older woman said she saw a beautiful girl run from the apartment. And it didn't even cross her mind when we were there. But when they showed her Emma's picture..."

I wasn't in disbelief that Emma was involved. But I was surprised it had all been wrapped up. "I honestly thought you were going to come in and tell me they'd locked up Mickey." I thought for a moment. "So that means she was involved with her grandmother and the two cousins all along?"

Alex nodded. "It looks that way."

"Even the mother?"

Melinda looked from me to Alex. "I never imagined there was so much to all of this."

"Always," I said, turning to Alex. "Melinda's moving away."

Alex looked like she tried to hold back a smile. "That's great," she said, and asked Melinda where she was heading.

Melinda said, "Well, I have a cousin out in California."

Alex picked up the envelope in the middle of the table. "What's this?"

"That's the money I owed you," Melinda said. "I wish I could pay you more, but—"

"We told you there'd be no fee," Alex said.

Melinda grinned. "I appreciate that. But I want you to have it. You both deserve it. You're an incredible team." She looked from me to Alex. "There's something special between you two. You deserve each other." She stood up from her seat and stepped toward Alex. "I really mean that." Alex stood and gave Melinda a hug. Melinda said, "Thank you so much. You're amazing."

I got up and stepped toward Melinda, for a moment unsure if I deserved a hug myself. But she wrapped her arms around me and gave me a kiss on the cheek. Into my ear, she whispered, "Take good care of Alex. I know how you feel about her."

As we let go, Alex and I watched Melinda walk out the front door.

We sat back in our chairs, and stayed quiet. I don't think either of us knew what to say.

Alex handed me the envelope and I stuffed it in my pocket. "I'd better get home. Raz has been at the neighbor's house since yesterday." She stood up from her chair. "Do you want to come with me?"

I stayed in my chair, looking up at her. "I think I need a nap."

"Since when do you take naps?"

I shrugged. "I'm thinking about starting."

She smiled and reached for my hand, pulled me up from the chair. "Come on. Raz will be happy to see you. Maybe he'll take a nap with you on my hammock."

• • • • • • • • • •

Thank you for reading *Dead in the Creek*. If you enjoyed the mystery, please leave a review wherever you purchased your book.

Ready for more? The Henry Walsh series continues with *Dropped Dead*. Visit GregoryPayette.com

Half Cocked
Danny Womack's .38